The Broncobusters

By Anna Elizabeth Judd

Table of Contents

Paperback ISBN: 978-1-7335551-4-2
Hardcover ISBN: 978-1-64873-183-9
Ebook ISBN: 9781952274114

Printed in the United States of America

Published by:
Writer's Publishing House
Prescott, Az 86301

Cover and Interior Design by Creative Artistic Excellence Marketing. Project Management and Book Launch by Creative Artistic Excellence Marketing https://lizzymcnett.com

Preface:

The **Horse**

The Brilliance of Your Stature

Creates an Image of Perfection

Floating Throughout the Land

Free to Roam in the Face of Adversity

Your Strength Shines Through

From Every Fiber of Your Being

With a Heart of Fire

Passion to Survive the Existence of Time

Your Chi Flows in a Glow

Infusing Life's Energy

To the Beings in Your Presence

Through Evolution You Became Extinct

Your Image Silenced from Sight

Although the Essence of Your Soul

Placed in the Ground to Flourish

Once Again. Recognized as,

"The Grass Remembers Them."

Review of The Broncobuster's - By Scott Francis Davis

The Broncobuster's is included in the vast troves of western novels depicting the "Cowboy Way," Horse Whispers, Gunslingers, and the Wild West, but very few scratch the surface relative to the vibrant depictions through which Anna takes this storyline.

Images of cattle trails and round pens all come to life courtesy of Judd's incredible first written venture. You don't need to be a horseman to like Anna to get the full picture of how life in the Old Frontier use to be...she affords that through her incredible story-telling!

The Broncobuster you leave you wanting to read more of Judd's westerns novels. Coming soon…… The Hourglass of el Diablo. Anna provides it all, as if you yourself are in the saddle along for the journey. This is one of those rare books that comes along where readers from nearly every genre can appreciate and enjoy. So read, *The Broncobuster*…and enjoy the trip through time!

Acknowledgements

Horsemen are exposed to inclement weather; hot summer heat, stinging sweat in the eyes, and spring mud up to the knees. Not to mention breaking the ice on the water pails, snow falling, and ice storms. But these inconveniences pale compared to the spiritual enlightenment that is received by spending every day with a horse.

Competent trainers have passion in their hearts for horses. Horsemanship is learned in a multitude of fashions, but guidance from an Equestrian Professional is the key to success. For example, I had the privilege of being instructed by two World Hall of Fame trainers: Pete Kyle and

Lighting Leonard Moore. They taught me the art of patience and perfection, two things that are a constant struggle when handling horses. Below is a literary reference that has given me insight when handling a horse.

"In any question of wisdom or prudence which the king put to them, he found them ten times better than all the magicians and enchanters in his kingdom."

Daniel 1: 20

In my vast years of training, there was one characteristic that remained consistent with horses, either young or old. Equus is a herd animal, therefore the fight-or-flight instinct is their basis for survival. Training must follow the patterns of natural instincts. When the lessons stray, abuse becomes the foundation. Even though man domesticated Equus around 4000 B.C., there were sixty million years of evolution. Predispositions do not fade overnight.

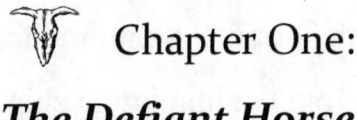 Chapter One:

The Defiant Horse

In the West, cacti grow abundantly while trees remain scarce. The hills become mountains when you are chasing a cow across the Sonora southwest. As the ground clears from the lack of rainfall in the summers, small thickets of shrubbery get so dense it's hard to see where they start and stop. These are the areas where the hardiest of wild cows survive and are the most difficult to catch.

My family settled in this valley after moving west with one of the great covered wagon caravans. With Mathew John, the name that was chosen for the first son, a custom was established when we arrived in the United States. Fourteen members of the original Spinhirne family departed from the immigrant ship. My mother has it written in the Bible; each generation writes their part inside the cover. My name is now the last branch of our tree. Most of my uncles died fighting in the war. The last died during a rash of fever that swept through the valley.

The relatives who settled here farmed. Their animals were used for work and running the ranch. Grandpa understood and nurtured Dad's passion for horses. He always said, "You never know where it comes from, or where it goes. The spirit just becomes part of your soul."

He began his taming career at age sixteen. Dad loved the wild cow hunt, so training meant riding a horse and working cattle every day. A tamer's salary was double that of cowhands. He worked hard and cherished traveling the countryside. It gave him time to sow his oats before he married and settled down to raise a family. However, when my grandparents passed, he had to take over the ranch.

Dad paid attention as a young lad to Grandpa's teachings. He knew how to farm, but preferred breeding horses. After few good years of farming, he earned enough money to purchase the southern section of land. It has a vast valley and stream that runs through the bottom. A suitable water source for the animals is essential during the summer months when rain is scarce. The adjacent pasture land is perfect for raising any livestock.

My grandfather worked hard to formulate solid relationships with surrounding neighbors. In return, the property was held for purchase. Grandpa never wanted the property for himself; he had it earmarked for Dad. A grand celebration took place when we bought the acreage. From then on, Dad set his sights on finding excellent bloodlines. One advantage of raising superior animals is they are sought after at auction. A key to producing excellence is good mares and stallions, yielding extraordinary foals. It requires weeding out the mediocre yearlings and only using the best colts for breeding. They are separated and sold at auction. Even Dad's second tier brought premium prices. His reputation spread far and wide. The tedious part, however, was maintaining superb bloodlines. Any breeder needs to retain a plethora of choices. Dad preferred to acquisition his stallions during late spring. That's when the horses are out of the gangly stage and becoming mature adults. The choice was a personal decision.

The new colts that are born replace the older stallions as they age and their fertility fades. During the last several years, finding acceptable replacements has been difficult. Our old stud, while still dominant at his age, raised concern. One Sunday afternoon toward the end of March, we got word a neighbor had a renegade colt he wanted to sell. The alert set forth was Dad's cue. We took a drive, and it was love at first sight. He found the perfect addition. His name was Rebel, and for obvious reasons, it suited him.

We had several maiden mares ready for breeding in the spring, and the black stallion complemented them. I still remember the day we brought him home, tied to the buckboard, ears pinned and every muscle tense with anger. Dad loved the high-spirited horses. Raising cattle was a dangerous profession and required a hardy mount to survive.

Most of these steers never see humans, except during the round-up. The bulls are territorial and will defend their domain.

There is an unexplainable rush chasing wild cows across the desert on a horse with a mind of his own. The drama increases when an angry cow chooses to protect her young in the midst of driving the bull. High alert and fast-paced is an understatement, and this life is not for everyone. It took a long time to determine my role as a tamer. It wasn't until the day we brought Rebel home that my true destiny surfaced. The fire and drive in his soul fueled my passion.

We had our work cut out for us that year. Rebel had to be under saddle and working cattle before the breeding season ended. If his talents didn't match his heart, then producing foals was pointless. Unlike most men, Dad learned his training skills as a tamer from the Indians. The colts took longer from the start, but the results were incredible. Cowboy ranchers spend most of their time alone on the range. The idea of riding a broken horse surpasses my idea of comfort. When started correctly they will stand and fight when necessary. Horses have a sixth sense for survival and reading cows. When a steed is taught to think, he works with a rider, being able to read a bull before the cowhand realizes what happened. The decisions could decide life or death.

Once the stallion's talents are proven, he is used to cover a few mares. The second-string stock are bred first. It will show how well the stallion transfers his genetics. The daunting phase is waiting around for the colts in spring. Winter exceeds my patience; the months are spent pacing the floor. The first ride out is exasperating. The anticipation continues while you ride past the line of trees and thick vegetation bordering the drive. Penned up from the weather, we are eager to stretch our legs. Dad could be aggravating at times, his fortitude solid and stable. When my impatience surfaced, he'd grin and taunt my haste. Then want emerged, and we'd race to open pasture.

The sound of horse hooves brought the herd to full attention. Mares stood alert, and the foals appeared to witness the event. Dad smiled, "Do you see the colt, Mathew?"

"Yes, but how can you tell it's a colt?" I never figured out how he knew.

"Mathew," he told me, "you should know better than to question me." A closer view of the horses proved his initial assessment. The young black horse was the spitting image of his sire. Dad lit up with joy. "We'll come back this afternoon before chores and round these two up."

"Alright," I replied. We finished inspecting the herd and counted about ten new colts on the ground.

Horse taming is not easy, but when the foals are handled at a young age, it lessens the task. That part is called imprinting. We handle the babies daily for a few weeks, then return them to pasture.

Over the past few years, our cattle herds grew, and we were running out of room. Before we started branding or separating for market that year, new pens had to be completed. On our first stock check, we found several calves injured. To treat them, we had to move panels inside the barn for shelter from the weather. Dad put most of the ranch hands to work clearing and sorting while they waited for me to return from town with supplies. He and Walter set off to doctor the hurt animals. One calf we rescued had the worst injuries. The wounds had weakened him, so he laid down much of the day. The prognosis looked bleak, but as long as he had the endurance to survive, we kept treating him.

There was so much commotion from the back pens that morning no one noticed the ruckus in the barn. Mended from his gashes, our young bull escaped his captivity and wandered off, frolicking with the other animals. His antics sent his mother into a frenzy, but unconcerned about his mother's distress, the cavorting continued. As his distance expanded, so did her anxiety.

After the sound inside amplified enough, everything stopped. Cowhands were on full alert. Dad cautiously entered the barn and surveyed what was going on. When Molly's calf did a Houdini, she panicked and tried to break free, wedging her horns in the railing. Her determination to break free caused the commotion. To calm the

cranky mother, they had to catch the calf.
At that point, it was safer to move the
panels. A dangerous task either way.

The men rounded up grain buckets and fed
the animals. Once everyone calmed down,
snagging the escapee was easy. Since Dad
was comfortable at Molly's head, Walter
took apart every panel. Nonessential
personnel waited outside just in case hell
broke loose. Each section had four pins
per slot, and removing them was time-
consuming.

He finished quicker than anticipated; they
were both relieved. Molly stood patiently
for the duration, but as the pressure from
the panels released, she grew anxious. Dad
had her head controlled for the moment, so

Walter was able to finish with the pins before she started to fight. But, his foot caught under the feeder as he pulled the last section. Dad had to drop the grain bucket, releasing Molly. She thrashed, swinging her head to break free from the corner. Walter was pinned by the feeder and fought to get his foot loose.

Seconds count when dealing with a raging cow, especially if a calf is involved. As the situation intensified, Molly's aggression grew. Dad struggled to regain control with grain, but the efforts were failing. Coercion drove Molly to shove the feeder forward enough that Walter was able to get his boot freed. As a result, she broke loose and bolted for her calf. Dad witnessed the incident as it played out. He grabbed Walter by the shirt, and the whirling stampede shoved him to the ground, but Walter was safe. Dad's actions saved one man but cost him his own life. He died instantly.

Words cannot ease the pain. The loss was unbearable. Loneliness creeped in and made itself at home. Time is the cure for agony. The only consolation was that Mom had passed many years ago, and Dad had missed her beyond description. They were grade school sweethearts and love never fades. Buried on top of the hill in the family cemetery, they could now both oversee the ranch for eternity. The universe stopped for me that day; burial is so final.

As I rode home, the sun set low on the horizon. It turned the sky into a magnificent array of colors. Life is an unyielding partner; it never pauses for our existence, only passing without hesitation. No one should be alone. The loss alerted me to a new appreciation of what my father went through since Mom died. Seasons passed, and time moved forward. The winters were less monotonous. Death has a way of aging people.

Over the nextseveral years the valley experienced a severe drought. We lost numerous animals during the winter. The first ride out in the spring validated our concerns: the green fields were now dried yellow weeds. Our apprehensions built as we rode, seeing no signs of life. It took most of a day to locate the stock. To our amazement, we found them in the southern section, a field filled with rich green grass. Our only conclusion to this mystery was an underground stream or river. We made it through the lack of rain without any further casualties. Alive and well, we breathed a sigh of relief.

My anticipation waxed when the black colt was not present, and the uneasy sense of loss settled in once again. Then a commotion stirred, titillated by suspense, the horses split, and a black stallion with white spots emerged. It was shocking to see spotted coloring in this part of the country. To my knowledge, colored stock came from the Indians. The event was a heart charging experience. Rebel had surpassed my expectations. Exhilaration filled my soul; Dad would have been proud.

Mesmerized by the markings, they shined like a copper penny in the sunlight. His name hit me: Cash. No pun intended, but he was worth every dime spent on the sire. Our silence broke as we rode back to the ranch, the stock healthy and our livelihood safe. It lifted our spirits, and a celebration was in order. Dinner greeted us with smiles and laughter, our hearts gay with opportunity. The next few days entailed health checks and branding the new horses.

We gathered the two-year-olds with ease, but locating Cash was another story. We searched every known hiding spot. With morning fading, the boys headed back while I continued to hunt for him. The foliage was thick, making it impossible to see, so for the second pass I paid close attention to the outskirts. Camouflaged by the greenery, hidden in the shadows, he stood baring his presence. The delay cost us most of the afternoon, so promptly formulating a plan was imperative.

The cove was perfect for capturing him, bordered by trees and shrubs, and only two exits: one where Cash was standing and the other behind me. The preferred choice was to drive him forward and block any outlets. In this case, the second-best option was to force a confrontation. If he gained his sire's heart, that should be an easy task. This plan was not without risk; incarceration brought on a fight, a wrangle that I deemed acceptable.

We braced for battle. The lasso circled high in the air as the storyline played out. It was mind over matter; the throw had to be perfect. A gentle tug and it firmly grasped the throatlatch. The dally had a snug fit, and the rope tightened for an instant. In the next few minutes, his intentions materialized. The ground shook; the sound of striking feet and gnashing teeth filled the air. I observed it all in slow motion. I prepped for impact, and everything stopped. Silence ensued, and it was a deafening quiet. Nothing moved, just utter stillness.

The suspense kept reality at bay. As the stun wore off clarity stirred, and life resumed. After a sigh of relief, we were still breathing. It took a few seconds before I could peel my hand from the saddle horn. Not one of my brightest moments, but problem solved. After a brief pause, he backed to a safe distance, and we stopped moving until he relaxed. For the meantime, things remained calm but, it was a tedious ride home.

We hit the south pasture with our final destination in sight. I noticed riders approaching; it was getting late, and they must have gotten worried. We were about twenty minutes from the ranch and our trek was almost complete. The minimal cuts and scrapes meant we had a good day.

Once they got close, I signaled them with a simple wave. They backed off and followed behind until we made it home.

We entered through the south side of the pasture leading into the newly completed back pens. Any wild mustang should be confined in a large area to start. They can be handled in a controlled environment. Once removed from the herd, instincts take precedence. It creates a dangerous situation for anyone who handles them, but it's the best setting for training purposes.

All hands were on deck and curious for details. I was itching to tell the tale and engage their eagerness. But, our jawing was interrupted when a buggy approached the house.

"Hold on boys, get the stock settled. I'll be right back," I said.

The wagon looked familiar. It was Conner, but it was strange for him to come out so late in the day. He was my dad's business partner before I was born. It was hard to see the details, but he had a passenger. My mind swirled trying to remember, but nothing registered. The vision standing before me so captivated my thoughts, only sounds resonated. Their meaning escaped my awareness.

"Mathew…. Mathew?" Conner said. My mind went blank.

After a few minutes of searching my memory banks, it flooded back. An image from fifteen years ago, a twiggy little kid. The girl had grown into a beautiful woman. Her dress a brilliant blue, it glowed in the twilight. Free from any decorations, the material flowed easily over the curvature of its frame. Long locks of brown hair dangled along the nape of her neck, wrapping around the delicate pearl necklace laying against her skin. Like before when I was fighting with Cash, my knees buckled, but there was no saddle horn at my fingertips to balance.

As the conscious ability returned, I realized how fifteen years can change a person. Her mother sent her to a boarding school on the East Coast. She was educated on proper etiquette, whatever that meant. No one person had ever captivated my attention like this beautiful woman. Seeing her brought clarity to the love my parents had for each other. Life alters destiny in the blink of an eye.

I heard Conner say for the second time, "Mathew… do you remember my daughter, Sarah?"

Cotton balls filled my mouth, stopping all speech. The only sound I uttered was, "Uhhhhh."

She smiled and said, "Hello Matthew, how are you this evening? It is nice to see you again."

A smile stretched across my face. My gut wrenched, butterflies did somersaults in my stomach, and I felt sweat pour from my skin. My head spun trying to form a response.

"Men endure fierce battles, yet beautiful women bring them to their knees and zap their strength in one fell swoop," I thought.

The encounter left me stupefied and utterly useless, a single interaction that lasted maybe five minutes. At this point, acknowledging her was moot. Hopefully, my reaction was acceptable.

Suddenly, we heard a crash behind the barn. Thinking to myself this was my ticket to run, someone yelled, "Mathew come quickly, we need your help!"

Thank God for the distraction. The commotion disrupted my chain of thought, and I was able to respond, "Sarah it's a pleasure to see you again."

The image of her face stuck square in my mind, a figure firmly implanted.

A well-placed diversion was spotted rounding the corner: Men atop the rail and Cash guarding the door. Horses are herd animals. When removed from natural surroundings the fight-or-flight instinct emerges. They become aggressive when their escape route vanishes. Instincts are what keep them alive. As the seasoned stock was brought inside to grain and stall,

Cash found himself alone in unfamiliar territory. His fear forced a confrontation.

The sight of them cowering from this wild beast tickled me. "Alright, boys, come now… you're not going to let this horse scare you on the fence?" I grinned.

Our skirmish that day in the cove had given me an advantage, and Cash was moved into the subordinate position. I became the dominant member of the herd. Proper taming trains them using their natural instincts. It is the most difficult lesson to understand and stay consistent. Our ranch stock is well trained and experienced with age, so to these cowhands starting a young horse was foreign. In this case, we killed two birds with one stone. School was in session for all parties.

My voice alerted Cash to my presence; he instantly whirled to face me. "Easy boy, come now let's talk," I told him.

The best way to minimize a confrontation is to avoid personal space - close the can of worms before a battle starts. The process takes time, and patience is the name of the game. We reached the entrance together, and he surveyed it and gleefully entered.

Cheers of adoration rang out behind me once the catastrophe was resolved. Until today, the men doubted my taming methods. In a way, I questioned my talents and knowledge as well. Since Dad passed, this was my first test as a ranch owner and tamer. Questions among the crew had surfaced many times over the last few months, and we lost several hands. It was an unforeseeable incident losing the ranch hands. Nevertheless, doubt was squashed tonight.

Feeling confident in my achievement, realization smacked me in the face. The reason I had desperately run for cover still waited in the driveway.

Suddenly, I felt nauseous, "Relax, breathe, deep breaths," I said to myself.

The distance gave me time to gather my thoughts.

"Sorry for the interruption. Our newest addition is headstrong…" My insolence registered mid-sentence. "Forgive my rudeness. Hello, Sarah, it's nice to see you again. Can I get you something to drink?"

Her voice cleansed my soul, "Lemonade is fine," she replied.

Conner left to handle business with the neighbors. We sat on the swing watching the sunset. During our conversation, sadness appeared in Sarah's voice. Her schooling on the East Coast opened countless doors of opportunity. Society was evolving, and women were becoming more than just nursemaids. Her passion fell into the realm of healing people. She'd been given a grant to enter medical school.

"A doctor," I said. "Isn't that a man's profession?"

She informed me the world was evolving; we didn't live in the Dark Ages any longer.

"What about children? The responsibilities are demanding," I stated.

"When did raising a family become the woman's responsibility?" Her voice became aggravated as she continued.

"Most people were raised that way. Myself for one," I replied.

"I know, but it's not right or easy…" There was an awkward silence. "I've been rude and inconsiderate of your hospitality.

My father should be back soon. I'll wait in the drive for him," she said.

"No… it's me that's sorry. You came here to talk, and I acted like an arrogant ass. Please forgive my indiscretion."

The conversation halted, she stood up and walked to the edge of the porch. There were no words to ease her aching heart.

"My father is coming. I apologize for any inconvenience. It was nice to see you again." Her voice cracked as she choked back tears.

She urged Conner to leave. He was puzzled by her eagerness to go, and that was understandable. I nodded my head and wished them a safe journey home. The incident left a gut-wrenching knot in my stomach.

I watched the buggy and noticed the whole ranch lit up from the moon and stars. What an incredible sight the sky was tonight. It reminded me of the times Dad, and I spent looking for animal shapes in the heavens, put there by God for us to enjoy.

My favorite constellation was Leo. Not only did seeing it mean the end of winter, but the Chinese believe Leo is a horse, not a lion. Yet, these thoughts faded, and my mind returned to the beauty that had brightened this ranch for a few hours. The pain in Sarah's heart was evident, and the actions of an idiot only served to make matters worse. Hopefully, a second chance might grant me the opportunity to change my insensitive behavior.

Lost in thought, Cash greeted me with a surprising snort, stopping me in my tracks. It was the last bed check before retiring. Just as words of disgust formed in my mind, a familiar sound rang out. One that no cowboy, horse or animal ever forgets. Between my feet, a rattler lay coiled, ready to strike at a moment's notice. In typical situations, a quick shot with a pistol and problem solved; unfortunately, it was hanging on the coat rack inside the house.

To see a snake travel this far was unusual, but seeing one among these animals was even more uncommon. The stock was getting restless as his warnings continued to echo off the walls. I watched closely to determine my next move. As the coil stretched out, lurching to strike in midair, I jumped to avoid the bite. When my attention was diverted, Cash struck the fatal blow. His attentive actions left me speechless once again. I closed the barn door and withdrew for the night. In the distance, I could hear a brief whinny, as if to say, "You're welcome." His humor tickled my fancy.

The usual routine was altered when sleep became more important than food. But, Stew, bless his heart, had left dinner on the table. However, taking the time to chew took more energy than my body retained.

The only appeal tonight was my bed; its relentless beckoning called my name.

The mattress cuddled and soothed my aching muscles, which accompanied by the added breeze felt heavenly. Although the snake was an eye-opening distraction, the incident with Sarah weighed heavily on my mind. Our conversation replayed many times in my head. The effect a woman has is unimaginable. Sleep ran from me like scared rats jumping ship.

Dawn emerged and roosters crowed promptly at five o'clock. Our daily routines were so ingrained that returning to slumber after sunrise did not happen. This morning was the exception until a familiar aroma beckoned: biscuits and gravy. Under normal circumstances, I would question how and where, but today was different. The scent was inviting; my stomach demanded nourishment. I was unable to ignore its commands, and hunger served to divert attention from my aching body.

On the table next to the dish was a note stating, "Don't assume all women are the same. We can take care of a family and handle a career. I thought you might enjoy a home-cooked meal. Signed, Sarah."

I scraped every morsel clean on the plate. It tasted like Mom's cooking. While I reveled in the aftertaste before drinking my coffee, a knock at the door disrupted my reverie.

"Mathew it's me, Rusty. You better come!" he said.

"Alright. What's wrong?" I asked.

"It's your horse again. He's got the boys pinned in the barn," he stated.

At the moment, the crisis seemed meaningless. Coffee was the only thing that mattered. The aroma teased my senses. "Ignore their demands, I trusted the sensation. They are grown, men. Cowhands, experienced cowboys," my brain taunted.

"Mathew, are you coming?" Rusty asked again.

"Yes, yes, let's go!" I replied in disgust. "Just once, a morning cup without interruption, is that too much to ask for?" I thought to myself.

Our hurried pace fueled my exasperation about leaving hot coffee on the table to get cold. However, I was utterly delighted when we entered the barn. The laughter rolled through instantly; the scene was purely ridiculous.

"Really, guys, for this?" I asked.

Rusty replied, "Mathew, please, what should we do?"

In the middle of the feed trough was the funniest thing I'd ever seen. Cash had taken advantage of his dominance over both stock and ranch hands. He was defending his loot. In this case, his morning oats. It was fair to assume his palate for grain demanded attention.

As I stood in the doorway, laughing at the sight before my eyes, Walter hollered, "Mathew, git that damn horse."

"Ok… come on Cash, let's go!" I calmly insisted.

To my amazement, he honored my request. His prints were all over the cookie jar.

Chapter Two

The Encounter

The talents of any cowboy worth his salt are tested when taming a defiant mustang. Indians called this "Horse Whispering." It trains them without breaking their spirit. The confirmation of your success may not be evident until a crisis occurs. Then the nature of your genius will expose itself. Since time is the only test that uncovers victory, my doubts ran deep. Failure could result in someone's death or injury, and either one of those outcomes is not preferable.

The spring cow hunt was only a few months away, and the impending chore hung over my head. Training Cash was my first endeavor without Dad. Our success was imperative, and a tremendous weight rested on my shoulders. We divvied the tasks up between our staff which enabled us to complete business ahead of schedule and just normal maintenance remained. Everyone slept better knowing the ranch was running smoothly. As the new boss, proving my role as owner was required. The men had their concerns and it takes a while to gain the trust of your employees. The validation, in this case, rested on my success with Cash. The clock ticked; time waited for no man.

By morning my anxiety welled up: testing my abilities began today. We hadn't told anyone else about our plan to lessen the stress. After breakfast the boys headed out, leaving us alone. Horses are tuned into any alteration in character, so keeping my composure was essential. Walter stayed with me, in case of trouble with Cash. He knew and believed in the methods taught by the Indians. Everyone else left to complete ranch work.

Behind the barn is a small circular pen, and inside stood a large railroad tie.   In the past, cowboys snubbed horses to the post and let them stand tied. They either quit fighting or broke their neck, whichever came first. It's termed breaking a horse, a tradition that extends back hundreds of years. But knowing and choosing are two different things. This cowboy uses humane methods to tame a colt. No sane man wants to ride a broken horse.

Unbeknown to Cash, our interaction in the pasture was the start of taming. His capture predisposed me as a dominant member of his herd. The most challenging lesson ended yesterday. It did not denote his absolute submission, since the smartest horses are the most arduous to train. The initial steps of taming begin in the circular enclosure. It allows the horse to move forward without the stress of restraint. The practice cultivates flight instincts, and when they are forced away, it draws forth their natural impulses.

Once I was accepted as a member, Cash would be determined to stay or fight, not to leave. After a few hours of maneuvering around the pen he followed rank. He became accepting of my presence. It was time to desensitize him with the touch of a rope, blanket, and saddle. If he didn't correlate being lassoed with fear, it should be easy. Two things might happen: the horse either accepts confinement or contests captivity. In a few seconds, a confirmation of the latter appeared. Cash fought the restraint. In these situations, the wrangler is committed to maintain dominance and win the battle.

The skirmish lasted almost an hour, and I squashed every attempt he made to regain control. His tightened muscles, widened stance and every toss of his head matched the striking hoof to the ground, challenging his restraint. It looked like a mouse being tossed around by a playful cat. Neither one of us were giving an inch to the opponent's requests.

Walter moved from sitting on the fence post to standing at the rail. It gave him a better vantage point to view the scuffle. As doubt emerged a glimmer of hope appeared; both of us were soaked in sweat and exhausted, but Cash faltered. He was ready to concede. We watched his feet, waiting for the faintest sign of movement, the motion would show victory. The whites of his eyes disappeared, and lowering his head meant success was in sight. Sometimes, winning the small battles outweighs everything.

As the fight drew to a close, the lariat dropped, and he stood relaxed. But the battle had tightened the lariat loop under his throatlatch and required some effort to be loosened. His lack of response to my hands on his jaw was unexpected. His progress was astonishing. As we ended the session, he moved to a close distance, following me to the gate. It was a step that ensured my dominance.

The boys finished work early and observed my taming beside the barn. We had kept our plans for the day quiet, as they believed the only way to train a mustang was to break them. Startled by the cheering ovation, I found the jury had ended their deliberation and concluded not guilty.

"Mathew, I watched your father tame many colts, but I believe you have surpassed his abilities," Walter stated.

Grateful, I replied, "I don't know if that's true. Maybe someday I might learn as much as he forgot." The tension I felt about proving myself vanished.

The boys sat on the rail and joined the conversation. It was morale boosting to chat about life. Cash, in the meantime, pushed his way into the conversation. With one leg cocked and his head over the fence, his apprehensions passed. His personality shined.

The day's victory carried on after dinner. We built a campfire and ate Stew's famous apple cobbler, and then we settled in while he entertained us with stories of his younger days. During the tales of woe, two guests arrived: Conner and our preacher. Saturday was the annual church social and dance.

Upon their leaving, Randy yelled, "Mathew is it true that it will be here at the Lonestar?"

"Yes," I replied. "Stop smiling and get to bed, we have a big day tomorrow."

By morning the butterflies returned to dance in my stomach. Today entailed saddling and riding. Whenever you mount a horse, anything can happen. The first few rides remain the most dangerous; with or without a rider, horses are agile. Time under saddle trains the riding stock.

Each day starts with a repeat of the earlier lesson. Since the join-up was complete, he was ready for the blanket and saddle. Only when fear subsides will the steed be content in the cowboy's presence. The session went well; he accepted everything in stride. It is a good sign when they are calm, relaxed and alert to their surroundings. His heart girth was deep and thick, a great feature for a cow horse. The cinch was attached and free from any pinching. His body posture remained accepting and peaceful, another sign of submission.

Before the horse is haltered or bitted, urging them to move saddled will decrease incidents while riding. He eased into a steady gait. It was imperative that he not feel pressured or traumatized at this point; otherwise he could associate the saddle with a negative action.

Each cowboy has their own preferences, so the next step will vary. There are men who bit a horse immediately while others work them haltered during the initial rides. My personal choice is the latter. One piece of stimulant at a time, small steps, and keep the taming moving in a positive direction.

The final leg of submission is haltering. Confinement removes the ability to flee dangerous situations. To minimize the threat, steps must be administered gradually.

The biggest hurdle is avoiding the flight mechanism once you gain submission. While the steed stands in the center, work your hands over his body, desensitizing them to touch and movement. Once comfortable they can be haltered, and that is how a horse is led.

Cash exceeded every expectation and we moved into the home stretch: mounting for the first time. He moved with the saddle and stirrups flopping, which simulates activity while in motion. Now, it was just a matter of carrying a rider. But, as I suspected, he made one last-ditch effort before total surrender. "Boy-howdy that horse could buck!" After three or four bone-jarring jumps, he gave up the fight. Cash came to a standstill and waited for instructions from the rider. At this point, the space was confining, and we both felt uncomfortable after the rodeo stopped. Nodding to Walter, he unlatched the gate and we strolled into the branding pens. After a few passes, Cash took a deep sigh, relaxed with his rider and we ended the session. Each lesson should stop on a positive note; never leave them in distress. Fear eliminates trust. A horse should always follow the dominant herd member. Our conclusion for the day was me walking proudly with an honorable mustang in tow.

Chapter Three
Old Roan

The ranch bustled this time of year, between the church social and round-up. Our new pens were complete so we began branding the young calves. Once the stragglers are rounded up, we move out for St. Louis. It's a four-month drive from the ranch. Cash was coming along nicely, but not prepped for the cow hunt yet, although he was getting closer each day. It was essential to have every good mount we had ready and healthy.

When our cowhands returned without Rusty that afternoon, the news was unsettling. Shiloh had been wounded by a piece of downed barbed wire in the north section. Rusty took his mounts seriously and his concern for their safety was admirable. He walked Shiloh home. While the wounds were not life-threatening, it knocked him out for a few weeks. To protect our riding stock, we rotated horses every other day. The shortage meant breaking in our newbies earlier than expected.

 Branding is one of the most grueling parts of ranching. The cattle must be stamped before round-up. Our strain increases with the rainy season. So, between the stench of burning flesh, mud and bellowing calves, we are glad when it's finished and peace resumes.

The day was long but productive. It ended with chatting with the men, a much-needed surprise. Parked on the rail with Cash we listened to tales. Then a familiar scent floated through the air.

Our banter paused. "Do you smell… What is that?" Rusty inquired.

"Of course, it's cornbread," Walter replied.

The conversation was entertaining, but food was deemed more important. Right on cue, the dinner bell rang. The crew hurried to the chuck wagon, but not without noticing one member of the staff was dejected from our departure. Cash stood nickering, yearning for us to return. The sight brought smiles.

Life travels in directions only the Creator can decide. Sometimes we tend to forget the little things that make living worthwhile. A cowboy's profession isn't glamorous and at times it's very lonely. We spend most of our days alone on the range with only a horse for companionship. Now, while I cherish the mounts on this ranch, human contact is necessary. The cattle drive and market auctions happen once a year and take the better part of four months, so we spend the last few weeks before departure with family.

As a celebration for the church social, Stew makes his famous cornbread. The entire town relishes the delicacy, but it also means his wife visits. Bernice, his wife, had stayed with me after Dad passed. Her help was invaluable, but the memories were still fresh and painful when I saw her. Bit in this case, the sorrow was worth every penny. She is an incredible woman.

We ate dinner and celebrated the victory with Cash today, but then on cue, "Mathew, are you heading to town? Time is a wasting boy!" Stew yelled.

"Yes, leaving now, Stew, straight away," I replied.

The ride to town was uneventful, except for the images of Sarah running through my mind. The face of an angel captivated my attention.

Bernice's arrival corresponded with mine, thank goodness. Stew would skin me for any delays. We greeted each other and loaded her luggage, after which she requested to make a personal stop at the mercantile.

I replied, "Of course, as long as you explain to Stew the reason for our delay."

"You have my word; I'll only be a few moments."

The sadness I expected was minimal. Instead, her presence lifted my sorrow, replacing it with joy. It was an unexpected delight. The agony of losing a parent welled deep in my soul. She had been a blessing in our lives, and it would be nice to spend time with her again.

Bernice returned with a small package. The box was addressed to me. "It is for you. Your mother asked me to hold it until the right time," she stated.

Inside was a wedding band. "This ring belonged to your mother; she entrusted me with it after her death. I was to pass it along when you were ready. Mathew, she would have given anything to be here with you today. She loved you."

"Thank you, Bernice. The ring is beautiful. I hope Sarah accepts it from me."

Tears rolled down her cheeks, "I believe she will do just that."

The last year had been challenging with losing my father. We became close after Mom died. At times, the loneliness was agonizing. The idea of growing old with someone seemed more important every year that passed. With my mother's ring and parents' blessing, the decision was easy.

Life brings forth new opportunities each day. Mine began after receiving that package. The ring was a symbol of unity, oneness. In one fell swoop, my destiny was clear. The cares, concerns and worries of the past and present vanished. My doubts were eliminated; Sarah would become my wife.

It was an incredible evening. The crisp snap in the air meant spring was making one final stand. We could feel the chill on our cheeks as the horse trotted along. Bernice snuggled next to me, trying to stay warm. My mind drifted, eager for the day Sarah sat at my side. The sensation was comfortable.

The sound of the crackling fire echoed throughout the ranch as we rode in from town. Everyone had settled down, laughing and talking. Their conversations caused them not to notice our arrival, and it warmed our hearts to be part of this wonderful family. Neither of us wanted to disturb the scene. The revelers' merrymaking lasted late into the night. Since the church social happens only once a year, I gave them Saturday to rest and celebrate. The entire town and surrounding valley participated. The ranch hands would be worthless due to the festivities. It doubled my workload, but seeing them having fun was worth the extra chores. My only request was one cup of coffee without interruption.

Sleep left my bed that night. My thoughts raced, not unlike a mule stuck in reverse. Visions of my future bride ran around and around. Being a cowboy was easy. The words to convey my emotions were non-existent. The only solution to my predicament was a hot cup of coffee and time to think about things and bring the battle in my head to a halt.

The scent of the fresh brew gently permeated the house. It eliminated any thoughts about returning to sleep. Just the aroma teased my senses. Ready to receive its pleasure, my lips rested firmly on the mug, waiting for the warmth to awaken my tired body. The gradual tip of the mug forced the liquid gold to pour from its container. Eager to taste the heavenly mixture, my plan was halted when a disrupting intrusion occurred, "Knock, knock."

The first sip was shredded to pieces. "Just one drink in peace, is that too much to ask?" I thought to myself. "Come on in!" I hollered.

The door opened, and Bernice peeked inside. "Mathew, are you dressed yet?" she asked.

"Yes, what can I do for you?"

"We need to set up tables for the baked goods."

"Be right there, Bernice." My initial plan for the day failed, but maybe the second one would keep my thoughts at bay?

Assisting the ladies with table preparation took some time, which delayed breakfast for the stock. My tardiness was promptly addressed. Cash continued to remind me of the error while I was making rounds. The world revolved around him.

The highlight event for the church social was the match race. Horses from around the country arrived to compete. Rumor of a new contestant from St. Paul brought curiosity to a head. They were claiming he beat Old Sorrel. Any horse that can trounce Old Sorrel must be witnessed. There was no time to waste: The race started at one o'clock. Rusty was warming up Old Roan in the pasture behind the barn. The earlier delay left me running late.

As I darted for the start line, someone yelled, "Mathew wait! Mathew."

The voice sounded familiar, but the commotion masked it somewhat. I contemplated stopping and seeing who was calling, but my eagerness remained in charge. Then, a second call rang out. "Mathew, please wait!"

My pace halted when I heard the voice more clearly. The world stopped; silence ensued. A tingling sensation ran up my spine. Upon turning to greet her, my eyes fixated on Sarah's hand as it connected with mine. There was no preparation for this moment. My emotions left me speechless once again.

"Can I join you for the race?" she asked. "Has it started?"

Still stunned by her arrival, I nodded my head yes and stated, "Let's Go! Quickly."

Joy entered my soul. God had returned the woman of my dreams. Entranced by the encounter, we watched the race.

The rumor drew in record crowds. Most of them wondered if a new winner would be announced today. Old Roan was energized this morning. Somehow, he knew when it was race time. The competition fueled his soul. He loved to run.

The announcer stated, "Everyone line up. Get ready." The gun was raised, "Bang!" The race began.

Called by the announcer:

"And they're off. Down the stretch, we have the new chestnut and Old Roan leading the pack. Following close in third is Old Gray; hot on his heels is Little Blacky. Cinnamon is coming on hard. In front, Old Roan and the chestnut are digging in hard for Weavers Pass. It's a tight turn. Now, coming in for the home stretch, we have Little Blacky passing Old Gray. Cinnamon is taking third place and pushing hard. Neither lead horse is waning. No winner yet! The Crowd Cheers. Racers are just passing the halfway mark. Old Roan is holding his own… Oh wait, damn! Old Roan is falling back; the new horse is making his move."

"Push him, push him!" I yelled.

Rusty hunkered down, and his horse's ears went back and his nose poked out.

Determination took full force. They drove hard to the finish line. We watched as the horses drew near, still neck-in-neck.

The announcer:

"Can Old Roan hold the pace? It's a tough call. Both are battling to the end." The crowd watched carefully as the horses crossed the white line.

Old Roan was no stranger to match races. It was unexpected, as his presence normally intimidated the competition. Any horse that could beat him must be seen up close, met in person. Old Roan and his rider's heads hung low as sadness took over the team. They were crushed.

"Rusty, you did incredibly. We knew this day would come. It happened to be today. Let's find the stallion who won. They deserve our congratulations," I told him.

The search was short-lived. His owner was searching for us. "Hello," he said. "My name is Samuel Adams."

"I'm Mathew Spinhirne. It's nice to meet you. That is one fine animal. What is his name?"

"Steel Dust," he said.

"Steel Dust- Wait, *the* Steel Dust?" He nodded and smiled at my surprise. "I am thrilled to see he exists. Some think he's a myth. Please stay and have dinner with us, or just stay the night. I'll give you a tour tomorrow." Eagerly I waited for his response.

"Mathew, I'm the one who is honored. Your father's horses are legendary. When word got out that the match race was at the Lonestar it was a done deal. I had to see for myself."

I was surprised by his statement. "Your father tamed the stallion Rebel," he said.

"Rebel? That was a long time ago. The third-year foals will be hitting the ground soon. We do, however, have one of his first colts in the barn: Cash; he is riding age."

"I'd love to see him, Mathew. Thank you," he replied. Our jaunt was delayed by reminiscers of losing the race.

After which we walked into the barn where Cash was stabled, "Mathew, he is exquisite. You should be proud. The balance, muscle tone, and intelligence are exciting. A good horse is hard to find. I'm impressed."

During our conversation, Cash moseyed his way over to the fence and joined our dialog. His usual antics surprised Samuel once again.

"Mathew, how did you do this? He's so friendly, and wants to be here with us," he said.

"That's a question waiting to be answered. I don't know if it's the horse or training."

"Whatever you have done, keep doing it. Please, let me know when you figure it out."

"I promise," I stated.

With Samuel cleaning up in the house, I needed to find Conner and Sarah. After the race, assisting Samuel was time-consuming. We lost the race but found one of my dream horses. Steel Dust here at the ranch even for one night was an incredible experience.

Deep in thought and not paying attention, Conner saw me walk past him and the preacher. "Mathew, there you are. I've been looking for you all afternoon," Conner stated. "We saw you talking to the man who won the race. Do you know him?" he asked.

"I do now! He owns Steel Dust. His name is Samuel Adams, a wonderful person. He is staying the night and wants a tour of the ranch tomorrow. Apparently, word has spread about the unbreakable stallion. He came here to see for himself," I told him.

"That's wonderful Mathew. Let's catch up next week."

We finished chores as Stew rang the dinner bell. "Come on, we better run. Stew does not tolerate tardiness," I explained in an insistent voice.

"Lead the way, Mathew. Dinner sounds good, and I'm starving. You don't need to call me twice," Samuel answered.

We approached the tables, and a beautiful young woman with brown curls in her hair and a wide smile greeted me. "Mathew, I made a plate for you and saved a seat at our table." My heart jumped.

"Sir, can I get a plate for you?" Sarah asked.

"Yes, umm," he responded. "However, I don't believe we have been introduced yet."

"Oh- I am sorry where are my manners? Samuel, this is Sarah," I stated.

"Please gentlemen, follow me and I'll get another plate," she responded.

When everyone was seated, the preacher stood to say grace: "Bless us, O Lord, for these fine gifts we are about to receive from your bounty, through Christ our Lord, Amen." The crowd responded, "Amen."

We ate till our bellies were stuffed. The crowd quieted down and listened to the fiddle player. Music is soothing, at least in this case. My nervous feelings resumed upon seeing Sarah during dinner. I respectfully excused myself to retrieve the ring.

Sarah met me on the porch as she exited the house. "Mathew, can we talk privately for a few minutes?" she asked.

The last rays of sunlight illuminated Sarah's rosy skin. Speechless from her beauty, my mind wandered, lost in the moment. We gazed into each other's eyes, silent as the sun vanished below the horizon. Suddenly, words were not necessary.

She placed her hand on my cheek, "Please… forgive my actions from the other night, I was abrupt?"

"Shush," I said. "There is no reason to apologize."

I pulled the ring from my pocket. She held out her hand. "Sarah, I promise, to love you until the Lord takes my last breath if you will be my wife…"

It fit like a glove; she smiled. "Yes."

As the sounds of music floated throughout the ranch, we waltzed. It completed a day blessed by the heavens.

Chapter Four:
The Spirit that Lives Within

The sunrise brightened the sky of another beautiful day. My coffee was consumed without interruption, what an unexpected pleasure. Stew's breakfast bell rang right on time as usual. So far, everything flowed perfectly. Samuel was already seated at the table chatting with Stew when I arrived. He had woken at first light and went searching for some hot liquid gold.

"We've been talking about the ranch Mathew. I'm sorry about your parents. It's hard losing them so young. Stew tells me you have done an incredible job taking over for your father. The men love and respect you. It has been a worthwhile trip. Thank you for the hospitality," Samuel stated.

Words of a wise man. "A road forged free from obstacles is a path traveled without gaining wisdom. Hurdles are the key to success. Knowledge takes practice and commitment," I said.

"It's been our pleasure. You are welcome here anytime. Whenever you're ready for the tour, Rusty is saddling up now," I told him.

In the early morning and evening, the horses will water and then move to high ground for added safety. A good vantage point helps protect them from predators.

We headed for the stream by the cove, where we found Cash.

"Mathew, your family, has built a beautiful place. This acreage is prime property: rich grass pastures and a plentiful water source. You've impressed me again."

"As Stew informed you, my grandparents bought this land before I was born. My father purchased the last section before he passed away. We worked this ranch for many years together, but taking over as the boss has had its challenges," I stated.

We could hear the horses in the distance as we approached the cove. Rebel alerted us to his presence once we were in sight.

He's protective of the herd when other stallions are present. Rebel's majestic allure radiated from him. His black coat glistened in the sun. The safest bet was to admire him from afar.

"I have seen what was necessary to conclude my business here. This stallion's reputation precedes him. His bloodlines will fit perfectly. I plan to expand and start a horse breeding farm. Between our two stallions, I believe we had the best genetics. How many two-year-olds do you have? I want to buy them," he asked.

"Currently we have about twenty head… You want them all?"

"Yes, is that a problem? I will pay you cash as soon as they are delivered," he replied.

The words jolted my heart. "No. We have a deal."

"Great! We can take care of the details before I leave in the morning. Now, how about we shake things up? Samuel asked.

"What'd you have in mind?" I asked.

"Switch horses? I'd love to try Cash out," he said.

I was shocked. The question turned me into a kid in a candy store with twenty-five cents. I took a deep breath, grabbed the saddle horn and swung my leg over the cantle.   Samuel laughed at me sitting there, with a smile that covered my face.

"Mathew, are you settled up there? Can we go?" he asked.

"Yes, I'm enjoying this experience," I replied.

The tour lasted all day, which made me happy. We could have ridden till next week. The day would be etched in my mind forever.

On our way back to the ranch, Samuel told me about his family. He was a teenager when they came to this country. His father, a cattle broker, worked for one of the largest businesses in the world. They traveled and purchased stock for breeding and the market, which is how he found the horses that created the Steel Dust bloodlines. Of all the ranches, in all the towns, in all the world, Samuel walked into mine. It was important for him to prove the rumor's validity of my father's grand horse flesh, he wanted to see reality for himself.

We discussed the transaction over dinner. Stew cooked up a fabulous meal as always. The next morning, we trekked to town, met with Conner and finalized the deal. On the ride back, he proposed a trade. He would assist with the drive, and I would teach him my training methods.

The words were heaven to my ears. We had a large herd this year and months of tedious work ahead of us. "Accepted, no need to offer twice. As for the training, it's a feeling, not an exact science. The basics are the same, but each horse is different," I explained.

"Mathew, that is a true gift. Only real tamers have that innate knowledge," he said.

Our new adventure was a match made in heaven; we were two peas in a pod. The last several days had been exhilarating. Yet, feelings of sorrow lingered in my mind. I missed Dad. An after-dinner walk was just what the doctor ordered. Under normal circumstances, tale-telling around the campfire was expected when we had a guest, but tonight some advice was in order. The ranching business kept us moving. Between the cow hunt, cattle drive and taming new stock, it was more work than ten full-time jobs. Dusk waned, and night settled in as I walked into the cemetery. A vibrant scent filled the air: flowers, roses. A rose bush had sprouted up behind mom's headstone. Shocked at the sight, it warmed my heart. Mom loved roses, she always had cut flowers on the dinner table.

"Mom, Dad, I've missed you. It's been too long..." I began.

Halfway back to the ranch, Conner and Bernice met me, worried something happened. Bernice knew where I had been: the one place solitude settled in deep. It was a good place to resolve life's issues. Time ceased to exist, questions turned to answers, and resolutions were conceived. My spirit was calm.

Sleep was once again a friend. Morning was a long way off, and silence reigned. Warmed, comfortable and content, early dawn found the sounds of my snoring. As the roosters crowed, attempting to penetrate my slumber, their boasting fell on deaf ears. A cool breeze flowed through the room, cooling the air and filling it with a strong odor. The harsh scent caused an extreme urgency to rouse my dozing. Irritation burned my nose, and suddenly relaxation became non-existent. I jumped to my feet, struggling to gain some composure. My head was spinning after being startled awake. I stumbled to the door, an investigation was necessary to solve the mystery.

In the courtyard, four young pups wrestled with an unwilling play-toy: a skunk. It raged and warned them against their taunting, but these warnings were ignored. The continuing harassment forced the issuance of an aromatic mist, and an adequate dose showered each pup. The skunk strolled off, confident over the victory. Its victims scattered, searching for relief from the stench. They were rolling, rubbing, and scratching trying to diffuse the odor but to no avail. Watching as innocent bystanders, the event left me with a bad taste; even my coffee had a tang. It was a lesson learned the hard way.

The skunk catastrophe ended with no further issues, only four pups were left groaning in discomfort for a few weeks. Though my sleep was abruptly ended, the day felt promising. The morning schedule was a date with Cash. All the recent activities had delayed the training for a few days. It was time to learn if he had retained the knowledge of previous lessons.

Samuel and Walter were eager to witness the results, and they stood watching our interactions. Since several days had passed, I decided a brief review was in order. Cash worked the rail to stretch his legs and warm up. He raced around, showing his spirit with a few bucks, hops and snorts. Once his playful antics were complete, my cue alerted him it was time to listen. His prompt response to commands made my heart gleam with pride. With a short intermission, the second ride was in order. I was satisfied with his progress.

The initial acceptance of a bit to a green colt can be alarming. It's best if they wear it alone for a brief period. Walter handed me the bridle through the fence, and Cash accepted the apparatus with some coaxing. He chomped, chewed and salivated as most colts do. We left him to adjust while saddling Steel with Samuel. By the time we went to check-up on the young steed, he was looking meek in the corner, accepting the metal bar attached to his face. Once confirmed his manner was intact, we proceeded to the back pens. Samuel was on guard if trouble arose. The beginning steps in reining a colt are teaching them to give to pressure. Horses naturally run from pressure, hence flight animals. With a gradual, steady pull on one rein, they will learn to turn in that direction. Once the request is obliged, releasing the tension teaches them to give willingly. Cash was a natural.

Once confident he was under control, Samuel quietly joined us. Many young stallions become uncontrollable in the presence of another mount when first under saddle. Especially when it pertains to other studs, the herd survival mechanism comes to life.

The morning exercise was a complete success. We chose to end on a positive note. One or two more days and Cash would be ready to work some steers. Boredom issues can be resolved by putting a colt to work immediately following the initial rides. As my parents always said, "If you have time to loaf, you're not working hard enough." A worthy lesson.

The determination of my talents became evident. It was a dream come true, and a ranch dedicated to raising horses did not lack merit. Mustangs were dropping like flies due to ill-practiced techniques of the range cowboy. Until recently most men just broke them. If it were killed or injured during training, they would be rounded-up another one. Many ranchers who tired of these practices fenced their land and collected the wild herds into their stock, thereby minimizing the problem. As the prices increased, mustang abuse would cease. They might become a commodity, but at least it would encourage humane treatment.

Changes in my life were materializing without any action taken from me, and the jubilation left me speechless. Samuel had made me an extraordinary offer, but it would take time for me to acknowledge it completely. My entire profession would be raising horses. No more cattle drives or wild cow hunts. A meeting with Conner was in order. We raised cows on this ranch, and it was our only livelihood at this point. Not to mention, I was marrying his daughter.

Our discussion over Samuel's proposal was lengthy, but ultimately it was a solid choice. The agreement would benefit all of us.

Conner's response was, "I think that is a great idea. If you like him that's good enough for me. I have already done some checking, and Samuel is an upstanding businessman. Safety is always the best option."

"You understand we won't raise cattle anymore, and it may cut into our profits for a while?" I asked.

"Mathew, you are marrying my daughter. If this means your life can be safer and have a greater chance to grow old together, nothing would please me more. Besides, this is what your father wanted for the ranch. We had this discussion many times, but he never had the chance to see it through. You have an opportunity, and I won't stand in the way of your destiny," Conner continued to explain.

"Alright, then I will have him contact you to make all the detailed arrangements. If there are any problems, please advise me," I told him.

The last hurdle to overcome were objections from the staff. Most of them didn't know anything but working cattle. But, it wasn't long before we had an overwhelming majority elated at the new opportunity. The change would be gradual over the next few years, giving anyone who was uncertain ample time to make other arrangements.

Our evening campfire entertained numerous questions about the coming changes, most of which there were no answers to right now. Nonetheless, every ranch hand was on board and pledged to serve with the spirit that lived within.

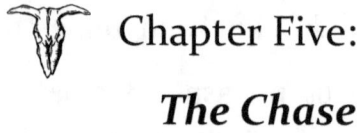 Chapter Five:

The Chase

By sundown, we packed our gear, repaired wagons and rounded up horses to move out at dawn. Tradition dictates the last night before the wild cow hunt and cattle drive we have one last meal as a group. The evening with family gave us comfort. It gives promise to the dangerous life led by a cowboy. The critical changes coming to this ranch made preparation a necessity. These concerns caused a distraction at dinner, and clearing my head was essential. It would be months until we returned home, and I didn't have time to worry about idle things. The new day waited for no man; business matters had to be settled before leaving.

By dawn, Samuel's men arrived, drained from traveling. So, for everyone's safety, we delayed our endeavor for another day. It allowed both stock and men to recoup. Planning for the long term was vital to our success. Mid-day broke before anyone laid eyes on them. Exhaustion was an understatement; they had traveled hundreds of miles in a brief period, almost the same distance as to the auction yards. We cleaned prepped and loaded their equipment for the next day.

Dawn peeked from the eastern sky, and our crew double checked everything. Any current issues had to be dealt with before we leave. Normally if the crew can have camp set up by noon, we stay on schedule. Then, we break into three groups to scout out the area and get a feel for the land.

At first light all parties fan out in a semi-circle, flanking the edges of the initial pasture. The maneuver drives the cattle inward to a central location where another group keeps them contained until they are joined with the main herd. Each unit includes one or two newbies, normally determined by matching personalities. Conflicts among the men get people killed, or at least injured, and neither is an option in my book. Accidents happen but being able to control these situations depends on your partners; whether that is a horse or human is irrelevant, lives are on the line.

Walter and Teacup, the youngest of our crew, rode with me. Many years ago, Teacup's father passed away when his horse stumbled in a gopher hole; he died instantly. The animal broke its leg and had to be put down. The scene is a ghastly sight that you never forget. After his death, Teacup's mama tried to keep him from the range, but there is something romantic about the wide-open spaces, its limitless trail becomes a permanent inhabitant.

Since then, Teacup had become one of my best hands. He has an innate nature with both cattle and horses. His size was especially helpful. The boy stood six feet four with shoulders as broad as a barn. Intimidation alone kept him safe most of the time.

The area we took was filled with an unusual amount of thicket brush; this undergrowth is excellent camouflage. There might be as many as four or five steers hiding in one coppice. We surround the section from three sides, driving them into the open and taking caution not to block the exit routes. Some of these old bulls will run right through a horse if cornered, so giving them space is important. Death is not worth the risk; gathering them later is the best option.

At the first thicket, Walter noticed movement. Teacup took point, and we fanned out. Standard placement is one on either side of the lead horse. When catching these renegade cows, everything is reversed (the healer, hence hind feet). The ropes are used first to slow their pace, then the hazer directs the header. He moves out to control the bull's direction, while the header lassoes the horns. The hind riata is released once the bull settles.

The point rider, Teacup, moved in to drive the group. Once they scattered, we could locate the dominant members. As each cow darted across the pasture, we noticed the old heifer. Her reputation was famous; she was Dad's favorite. Every year he left specific instructions to leave her alone.

She'd proven herself and deserved to live free until nature claimed her. In a typical situation we'd abide, but this time was different. All the wild cattle were headed for the auction yards.

Hellbent on freedom, she bolted across the pasture. Walter, wise to her habits, was the frontrunner. We stayed on the chase. But buried deep in my mind was a concern for Cash's mental state. I hooked both horns. He was young and inexperienced, but his concentration never faltered.

Once I had a solid hold of the head, Walter released the dally, and the fight engaged. In the distance, we heard her calf bellowing; this meant mama mode was in full force. Teacup, for the moment, had her young'un restrained. My header rope tightened down, and the dally secured. Cash came to a screeching halt when weight caught the end of the line. The tension made him quiver. We gently moved slightly to the right, keeping her off balance. Moving in a diagonal motion keeps the rope tight, helping to regain control of their head.

It is an excellent sign when the first cow of the hunt is caught with no complications. The initial catch just happened to be Dad's favorite. The battle raged on, each one fighting for yardage, neither willing to give an inch. A fevered froth of freedom reigned high in her mind, one that had gained her dominance in this herd. The feral look on her face brought tears to my eyes. My desire to capture her melted and my heart broke. I released the dally; it felt good. She earned her liberty.

Watching as she bolted for her calf, I heard Walter say, "Mathew, you know that cow was always your father's favorite? He would have approved, but only because he couldn't catch her either. He tried several times and ended up turning her loose just as you did."

"Really, he did?" I asked.

"Yes," he responded. She would prove her loyalty later.

The battle drained us; it was break time. We hunkered down for lunch and sat a while. The cease-fire would give all the cattle a chance to relax and ignore our presence once again. An ambush is best accomplished with surprise.

Re-grouping after we ate, Teacup took point. Why change something if it's not broken? We took our fixed positions in a triangle formation. Cash engaged the first steer to exit from the thicket. We overtook him with ease.

Ready to take the head shot, Walter hollered, "Get him, Mathew! Heel now! Don't hesitate."

I thought, "Heel him? I'm a header." Believe it or not, there is a big difference between a header and heeler. The header throws a riata over their head, whereas the heeler shoots for the ground.

The rope dropped just ahead of his back hooves, gathering both in the loop. Walter was ready, waiting for the steer to pause; he tossed but only caught one horn. Turning to holler for Teacup, right on cue, he hooked both.

When we have a good dally and they settle, the hind legs are released. The next few minutes required both horses to hold the steer. With no sign of submission, we decided to find a tree. Most cattle will not hurt themselves, but they have no problem goring a cowboy or the horse.

I eased out to give them space. Since Walter only had one horn hooked, Teacup had to take the lead with his rope dallied. He hollered, "Are you ready?"

Nodding, Walter released his dally. The steer continued to line Teacup out, but he matched his approach with a counter move. Stamina is the victor in this game.

Then, the worst happened, Teacup's lariat caught. My heart stopped as he worked to free it from the brush. His catch quickly gained control. The situation dictated we watch as bystanders. Instructions distract the cowboy and helping will get someone else hurt.

"Steady, Mathew," Walter said. "It's alright; he is a good hand. Give him a chance to work this out on his own. A good leader trusts his employees to make the right decisions. They know the risks. You can't blame yourself if someone gets hurt or killed. My experience exceeds twenty years, and nothing is worse than watching a man die, especially when you're the boss."

"Thanks Walter, that helps. You understand my position," I replied.

Finally, the rope freed itself, and Teacup regained control. Old Roan began to lather from exhaustion, but until he was secure, all we could do was watch. He worked back and forth across the field, gaining a few inches on each pass. Fatigue brings out the drive for freedom. By moving diagonally you gain an advantage, giving them less time to react. Cattle are not as cumbersome as they appear.

With the end in sight, ragged and fatigued, they reached their destination. Teacup had to shorten the distance between the tree and bull. When the process is done correctly, a bull will literally secure himself. Today the plan worked.

"Mathew," Teacup said, "that was a nightmare. He had me worried for a minute."

"You did just fine. I am proud of you. Your father would have been beaming with pride," I told him.

With the steer contained, we investigated for other inhabitants and found the area to be vacant. Grateful we were finished, it was time to rustle him up and end things for the day. Generally, after a few hours, they are willing to cooperate.

As we approached the tree, something appeared different. "Mathew... we are in the right place. I know this is right," Teacup stated.

"Are you sure?" I asked.

"Yes positive! Look- the tree, it's rubbed from the rope. He somehow got loose."

What happened remained a mystery. Our instincts jumped into high gear. We had an angry bull on the run. A quick prayer seemed appropriate. These are the times when a single mistake or distraction can get you killed. Trusting your partners, both human and animal, is imperative. Cash was proving to be an excellent cow horse. His instincts were strong. It gave me comfort having a good horse underneath me. They have senses out here in the open spaces we could never understand.

Seconds passed like molasses poured from a jar when hunting for these wild cows. There is zero room for error. In an instant, they can charge from a thicket seeking freedom. We'd made our way around this section full circle, and there was no sign of the steer. He could be injured or stuck with a riata dragging off his horns.

"Let's search this area again; he has to be here!" I stated.

In a triangle formation I took the lead, and we encroached the thicket brush. It was the largest in the area and closest to where he was tied off.

"Mathew, look!" Teacup shouted. "The rope end, on the ground." At the edge of the brush, the lariat was hooked on a branch. Wrapped tight, he would not go far.

Perplexed over the conundrum, we watched for movement, any sign of life within the thicket. Nothing… all remained quiet. Walter and Teacup expanded their distance between each other, opening the gap. Sometimes when you expose an escape route, it will initiate the engagement. The brush stayed calm, an eerie stillness. Eager to end this confrontation we edged our way forward, forcing pressure on the opponent. Unruffle, we continued the offensive.

Our movement finally got a reaction. The threat exposed a steamroller from within the center of the brush. Two cows with calves bolted from behind the steer, hellbent on the open pasture. Walter was hot on their heels. To keep order in chaos, he moved them to a safe distance.

The steer bared his intentions clearly: assault with a deadly weapon. He charged forward in the blink of an eye. The instincts of my partner gained priority, and Cash took ownership of his responsibilities. The pommel kept me balanced while seated deep in the saddle. I focused solely on the steer's actions and prayed for the knowledge to maintain control. My role as passenger held. The offensive ruled for the moment. But, only time would tell the conclusion.

Cash took a front seat in the first interaction. Our distance from the steer eliminated the possibility of roping his horns. The best course of action was to haze him toward Teacup, who braced for impact. Old Roan stood firm in his stance as the steer advanced.

Cash moved to the edge of his flank, a safer position to avoid the point of a horn. With his mind intent on retrieving the cows in his herd, we had to stay focused on the task at hand. If we faltered, it could all fail.

Teacup prepped, his lasso twirled high. Focused on the steer horns, it was a perfect catch. Old Roan backed to lengthen the space between them. The lariat tightened down, gripping the saddle horn. He had a solid hold on the bull.

Ready to disengage my stance, a sound rang from the bushes: wood cracking from intense pressure. Seconds later, the broken section of the branch flew through the air like a grenade. Everything became a blur. Sounds were muffled, nothing made sense. Everything grew dark; silence drifted in and the noise faded. Flashes of light illuminated the scene.

I woke, unsure of my whereabouts. The lighting was dim as if a veil covered my face. The scene looked familiar, but darkness masked everything. It looked like mom, my dog and me, but that meant I had died. I was in heaven.

While I tried to regain composure and clear my eyesight, an image knelt in front of me. She touched my face, "Mathew, I love you, please come back," her lips kissed my cheek, and she vanished.

My attempts to grab her hand failed, "No… don't go…" I cried.

Surrounded by emptiness, sadness rushed in. Intense emotions engulfed everything around me. Silence, utter silence. Time evaded the circumstances, with no acknowledgment whatsoever. I struggled to seek the outcome.

Bright spots entered my vision in pieces and things became clear. Finally, light once again illuminated life. The darkness dwindled. I gasped to breathe. The air was thick, like soup. I was dizzy, making standing impossible. As my dazed head cleared, a ringing sound took its place. The sickening unforgiving injuries of the happenings clung to my frame. I was still incoherent, and the idea of this pain subsiding fled town. So, the only option that remained intact was resolve this situation.

Nauseating soreness took over me, eliminating my ability to stand. Therefore, my survey of the scene had to take place as I lay on the ground while I regained my strength. The pasture was a dismal sight. A dead cow lay nearby. Remnants of some rope littered the field. But, the most upsetting was Teacup's horse lying motionless over yonder. Agony overtook my senses at the thought of losing Old Roan. I had to get up; his wellbeing was more important than my own.

I had strength to stand and walk for a few feet, and then I had to crawl. Time was of the essence, and reaching him was an absolute necessity. My endurance waned as I struggled to creep across the pasture. The drive to attain my goal ruled over my fatigue. I closed the distance and I had almost reached my destination. I was in such pain, but victory was in sight.

Old Roan's lifeless body twisted my gut. Completely helpless, yet I had to confirm the truth. Once I was close enough to feel his coat, my hand touched his side. Anticipation expected the chill of death, but instead, a sound emanated. He nickered. Joy flooded my heart. I held his reins for additional support while he stood. Gradually, we regained our bearings. The pasture was empty in all directions. Everyone had vanished. Then in the distance, I spotted something. My vision was still blurry, so I couldn't tell exactly who it was.

"Boy, are you alright? We need help," I asked him. Old Roan nodded.

I grabbed a stirrup and hit the saddle. His gait was wobbly, but he seemed sound. At this point, help was necessary. Urgency made the distance stretch as we closed in on the target. "Someone has to be here. They could not have just vanished," I told Old Roan.

The object appeared to be Cash; his white spots glowed in the sunlight. He looked sound, with no visible injuries.

"But what happened to Walter and Teacup, boy?" I asked Old Roan.

On high alert, scanning the area for other signs of life, a bellow sounded in the adjacent brush. We made our way to the thicket, and to my amazement, the steer was tied off to another tree. He seemed no worse for wear. Unsure of the situation and bewildered, we waited.

The pasture was silent. Confused, we needed answers. Then I heard, "Mathew, you're ALIVE!" Teacup yelled. He appeared from behind the undergrowth.

"Yes, and you're healthy," I stated.

"We thought you were dead!" He scanned my body for damage. After the inspection and satisfied of my survival, he hugged my neck. "Thank God, you are alright!"

"What the hell…. happened?" I asked.

"I am sorry Mathew. It's all my fault; the steer got free the first time. I should have known better and double-checked."

"No, it could have happened to anyone. I'm not blaming you." I told him. "But- what happened?"

"When the branch catapulted across the pasture, it pulled the bull sideways and I lost the dally. He charged Cash. From there I saw something amazing: that horse worked him. The steer was intent on hurting anything within reach. The plan worked perfectly until the second rope caught Cash's foot, pulling him down on top of you. It all happened so fast. The only choice was capture the bull and remove him from the situation.

"During the skirmish, you know my horse; he never balks from a fight. He was broadsided and went down. The bull darted across the field, heading for Walter and the cows. He had to be stopped. Cash appeared sound, so I mounted him, and we were in pursuit. I caught the rope right over there, and he chased me around the tree. There was no time to waste, Mathew. He already hurt you and Old Roan. I thought both of you were dead!"

"I know! You did a great job. We are all alive," I told him.

Walter, convinced the drama had died down, drove the cows into the center section of the pasture to reunite with the bull. Surprised to see us standing there in the open, he commented as to the whereabouts of the steer. After filling him in on the details, we sent Teacup to retrieve the old steer tied to the tree.

"Mathew, he's dead!" Teacup reported a few minutes later.

After careful inspection, the bull must have been kicked by one of the horses, causing internal damage severe enough to kill him. That proved Teacup had come much closer to death than he ever suspected, something I never shared with him. We finished the drive, and it was the last time any of us participated in the hunt for wild cows. The experience left us with a greater appreciation for life.

Chapter Six:

Market Time

East St. Louis Missouri, 1880s, more than a half a million head of
cattle were brought here, or to stock yards such as these. This made
cattle barons very wealthy.

Our ride home was a sobering journey; the three of us had cheated death. Not many people have that opportunity. There was grateful jubilation. Our new business venture was a blessing in disguise. Somehow it seemed God had a plan for the ranch and each piece of the puzzle fell into place. The situation brought reality to a head; we lived to survive another day. Without the fear of dying, we 'don't appreciate life, and we follow an unconscious routine, unaware that living is a gift.

Our task was a complete success with one exception, and the old cow deserved penance. Tomorrow we started the round-up process. The herd rested in the south pasture, giving everyone time to rest up and finish any necessities. Stew stocked the chuck wagons while the men dressed out a few steers for meat. Walter and Teacup made sure the horses were doctored and prepped for the four-month journey to auction. We would all enjoy this last night at home, as the 24/7 days ahead would take their toll.

Since everyone was busy finishing chores, it gave me time to grab supplies in town and see the doctor. When the steer charged and we went down, it broke some ribs. The incident left Teacup and Walter shook-up, so there was no need to make matters worse. They had enough on their plates without worrying about me. Our trek to auction extended over several months, and knowing the severity of my injuries seemed important.

The ranch was undergoing some significant changes which delayed our departure, making us the last drive in the valley to head out. During sale time, most of the businesses shut down. The stores were open half days and the motel closed but for a few hours in the evening. In other words, it became vacant around here. Conner and Sarah had left for St. Louis the day before; they would wait until we arrived in early August. Our local doctor, a great man, had delivered me when I was born. Since the town was quiet, he was headed for the ranch to stock medical supplies before morning. We passed each other.

"Am I glad to see you. We had a situation today that left me with some cracked ribs, or at least I hope that's all," I stated.

"Matthew, what are you doing riding? You should be in bed," he informed me.

"Please doc, just check and tape me up, I can't be down right now. We head out in the morning."

Under the circumstances, Bert, the owner of the mercantile, agreed to deliver the supplies. It saved us from having to run back and forth. The trade cost me a side of beef, but the courtesy was very beneficial. Dusk settled as we rode home. A cool crisp breeze gently floated through the air.

It was nice hearing crickets and utter peace. The next four months would leave me yearning for silence.

Night had a firm hold on the world when we got back. The place was quiet. Everyone had hit the hay early since we would head out at first light. The stillness was a bit unnerving. Even the house seemed empty until I noticed a lantern glowing in the kitchen. Stew, praise the Lord, had left dinner. The agony, however, drove me to lie down, but my stomach demanded food immediately. While seated at the table, my mind ran through flashbacks of the day. Facing one's mortality changes the way they think. Suddenly, you notice the birds singing, stars in the sky, or the smell of fresh flowers in the pasture. The idea of being grateful for pain was strange. The throbbing ache reminded me of the alternative, death.

Dinner refreshed my tired body and the aching subsided slightly. The hot cup of coffee was, however, the best conclusion to a long day. A decadent dessert, every sip deserving appreciation. Each sip tickled my tongue with its soothing warmth. While I looked at the last swallow, a notion hit. I had been able to drink the entire mug with no interruptions. The thought was an amusing way to end the day.

Once the pain from broken ribs and hunger subsided, a final check on Cash deemed necessary. Sometimes we get so caught up in our own lives that we forget about the animals. They endure the same stress we do and must be cared for as well.

The scene in the barn was definitely another one for the record books. Cash never ceased to amaze me. He was curled up on a large pile of hay, which he'd had to paw and dig, making it just perfect. Then once satisfied with the distribution, he plopped into the middle and proceeded to consume his bed. Admittedly, he had chosen the right menu item: rest.

With a slow, steady pace, the trip back to the house was long and grueling. Every muscle in my body was tightened and immobile. No wonder Cash had lay down to eat; standing hurt too bad. The old steer handed us a beating today. Bless his heart; he gave it all for freedom.

Morning hit, and the sun peeked over the horizon. Daylight poked through the windows. Temptation reared its ugly head, taunting me to move. It kept antagonizing me, nudging my subconscious to react. My sentencing was waylaid, as I was alerted to its intention. The verdict, however, allotted time to prep, since my position was preserved from the night before. While pondering the next course of action, someone knocked at the door.

"Mathew, are you alright? It's me, Dr. Webber," he stated.

I was never so glad to hear a knock. "Yes, please come in. I need some help," I yelled.

He noted his concerns. "I'm not happy with you getting out of bed with broken ribs," he explained sternly.

"Doc," I started to explain.

He interrupted me: "I know, you have to go, but don't say I didn't warn you. I informed Stew of your condition yesterday, and he will make sure you rest."

"I was trying to keep this quiet. They have enough on their plates."

"Ok… would you rather be dead? One of your ribs could puncture a lung.

Do you want to die like your father?" His statement alerted all my senses.

I hung my head and answered, "No."

"Just give it a few days, and then you should be okay. Stay back with the chuck wagon. Samuel and his boys are with you, so there is no shortage of help this year. Mathew, promise me you'll take it easy?" he pleaded.

"I promise." My dying over something stupid was the last thing we needed.

The next week gave harsh a new meaning. The demands of enduring my condition required a lot of energy. Although, hanging back with Stew made me realize how much work being the cook involves. Between preparing breakfast, lunch, and dinner, there is also stocking supplies, loading the wagon and setting up after we move each day. I owed him a debt of gratitude after this adventure, and maybe a raise?

Our group of wild outlaws settled down within a short period. We kept close track of their whereabouts. People always ask how you tell the cows apart when you have several thousand together. It's a strange question, but keeping count is part of the job. If cattle are missing, that means lost money.

It took a full week of hanging with Stew before the pain subsided and I began to feel normal again. Grateful for the extra help, he'd miss me in a few days when we were back to our regular routines. The change felt good. Secretly, it was like having Dad around, memories that will be cherished always.

The initial trail started with three rivers to forge. Cattle cross water in the open range, but when forced they balk every time. It was a nightmare, to say the least. Although, the late departure turned out to be a blessing: We were the only drive crossing the river. Plus, the drought meant that levels remained low. If we were lucky, we could have the herd through in a week, providing the weather cooperated and no stampedes erupted. Once the lead bulls start, the others follow suit in a split second.

Preparation to cross starts at daybreak when the stock is well rested. We divide them into several units, because groups are easier to maintain than the entire drove. Two men ride point, and their job is to stay ahead and scope out the terrain. It takes time and space to turn a drive of this size. Planning helps eliminate stampedes, a cowboy's worst nightmare. We move each group through, settle them down and proceed to the next. The camp is separated while the herd is crossing. If the traversing is halted for an extended period, pasture and water become scarce. Skinny or dead cows are worthless, so those delays force us to split and move to better resources. Not our preferred option, but necessary on occasion.

Walter took the lead. Today the river remained calm, and the weather was holding strong.

I gave the order, "All clear. Let's go." My commands are passed to the back of the herd. Each rider relays the message to the next cowboy behind them.

Chuck wagons, gear, and remuda are the first to move and set up camp. Each ranch-hand rotates between two and three horses a day. Cowboys riding tired horses have accidents. Cattle drives are a never-ending engagement, and during the night we have four cowhands on duty at one time. The only breaks are dinner and sleep. We can't even look forward to having a good meal. Our diet consists of beans, cornbread, and coffee. Twice a week, we have meat, and that is usually jerky. Baths come when it rains.

The dust is so thick from the cattle, it turns the sky brown. The drag men who travel behind the herd to keep stragglers moving along disappear. We put the young tenderfoots back there. They are inexperienced cowhands, and it's safest for them, and us.

The initial batch crossed the river with ease. Sure enough, the second group was a different story. One bull in the middle broke formation and bolted, the taste of freedom reigned high. We spotted him in a jiffy. My steed decided he liked chasing cows, whether I was in the saddle or not. In a few hundred yards the steer was pushed back in the herd.

Things rolled smoothly for the next few months, if a drive could be called easy. Normal incidents happened regularly, but minimal disruptions are expected. Well into the third month we crossed a dry patch of land and hidden beneath the dirt was a large mud wasp nest. The sky turned black, and the sound surpassed the noise of the cattle drive. Each man ducked for cover. Once the wranglers were on the outskirts, we pushed the cows into themselves. Being stuck in the middle will get you killed. The priority must be to eliminate every chance of a stampede before they start. Once it does, each cowhand is on their own; communication becomes nonexistent. However, in some instances everything happens so fast the only thing to do is pray.

Walter and I worked the front of the herd while Samuel stayed at the back. It is important for each member of your drive to know the rules, and who enforces them. The trail boss is in command, followed by the cook, and down the line with seniority.

The stampede led us to a canyon. We had to turn the lead bull, and this is no easy task when cattle are scared. Against my better judgment, lassoing him seemed necessary. The faster he reversed direction, the better. Walter and the men would have to follow suit as communication was impossible.

I took a deep breath and hoped for the best. The rope caught one horn and with a quick flip, both snared. The commotion behind me raged but moving him took precedent. Every additional step moved us closer to the gorge. The clock ticked, and he had to be pulled into the direct path of the stampede. It would cause a chain reaction, forcing the other cattle to change course. Once they turned, we'd need men along the ravine edge to push the others back into the herd. The foremost task was releasing him without getting trampled. My forte is not hazing, but today had to be the exception. To haze is run alongside the bull, lean over, and unhook the lariat.

The plan worked like a charm but pushing them to complete changing direction takes patience. We stayed on it for most of an hour, but every so often I caught a glimpse of the situation and it appeared, we were making progress. Once the drive turned, we rounded up the stragglers along the ravine edge. It gave everyone time to breathe and update themselves on our status. Gradually, the dust settled, and a visual inspection was possible.

Our efforts to control the stampede lasted for almost six hours until the herd calmed. The morning's casualty count: seven head of cattle dead, one horse severely injured, and a cowboy with a broken leg. We were lucky this time.

The only godsend was our final destination that day landed us in a great section of fresh grass and an adequate waterhole. Our exhaustion demanded rest for humans and stock. The boys dressed out the dead or severely wounded cattle while Stew set and bound Jessie's leg. After careful inspection, the horse's wounds were too severe and he had to be destroyed. Dad always said, men who were flippant about such things considered animals commodities, and they were not worth their salt.

An eerie silence fell over the camp as we walked into the vacant desert. My heart sank into the abyss. Nothingness filled the air; the only sound was of me gasping for breath. The steps hollowed out my soul, and emptiness took its place. Being trampled by a bull would hurt less. I prayed for some kind of intervention to eliminate this task from my fate. Only sorrow would result.

The pistol sat solidly in my hand awaiting instructions, but only the look of compassion came from the horse, staring back. His willingness to participate weighed heavy, and tears flowed from my eyes. I'd only observed my dad put down a horse but never completed the action on my own. It clarified that life is precious.

In the next few minutes, felt clarity and my request for divine intervention was answered. Passion for the existence of other creatures is a gift, one that entails great care and responsibility. No amount of excruciating agony excuses me from the job at hand. There is no accountability in cruelty, and leaving him to suffer is unacceptable behavior.

The shot echoed off the bluff surrounding the herd. Silence ensued, and my breathing returned. A solid ranch horse; his presence would be missed. Any loss of a family member, human or animal, is difficult. The impending quiet weighed heavily on my mind throughout the night. Several weeks passed before my sadness waned.

With all the river crossings passed, we had one last hurdle to overcome: Indian territory. It meant dangerous times ahead for the last month of our journey. As one of the latter drives to move through this area, it could go either way. They might ignore us or come ready to fight. My father taught me long ago to give them what they want and avoid any confrontations.

In most situations, the Indians are looking for compensation to cross their land. We drive thousands of cattle across their property every year; they are entitled. Some ranchers are greedy. The white man sure expects payment for what he owns. Fair is fair.

The new tenderfoots are ignorant about crossing Indian territory. There are rules to follow, and these decrees keep us alive. We had several hundred miles to travel. If we got lucky, our journey would proceed without difficulty. Everyone had to stick as close to the herd as possible and never wander off alone. We added lookouts to alternate from front to back and report anything unusual immediately. It would take approximately two weeks to traverse this area if we pushed hard, barring any complications with the drive. Ahead on the trail about a day and half ride was a waterhole, at which we had to stop for the better part of twenty-four hours. Any time stopped on Indian land is dangerous. On the second check the following morning, one point-man thought he spotted some braves, scouting the hills above us. We expected some movement, so for now, only the trail bosses were notified. Order had to be maintained, so alerting the whole camp was unwise.

Mid-day after our lunch break, a brave was noticed. Samuel and I opted to face the issue head-on and meet them ourselves. As we worked our way up the cliff side, my stomach jumped and twisted. Samuel remained confident we could negotiate a fair trade and guarantee safe travel.

With a few fumbled words exchanged, we met the chief. Not knowing what to expect, the experience was alarming. As we rode into the Indian village, the elders greeted us. One of the older men looked familiar. He spoke broken English, but enough to understand what he meant.

"The man called Mathew John, you know him? I see his features in your face," he said.

"Yes, he is my father," I answered. "What do you require as payment to cross your land?"

He responded, "The horse you ride, he is spotted. Where did he come from?"

Since his understanding of our language was limited, the response would be lengthy. "My father purchased his sire many years ago, from a man in our hometown. His dame is just a little black mustang mare, nothing special."

He nodded his head and asked, "Where did the mare horse come from?"

"My father purchased a small herd out of the south. His mother was one of those mares. She was bred to our stallion the following spring."

He replied again, "The horse you ride, it's colored. His bloodlines are Indian."

"Yes, I thought he might be," I stated to him.

"We don't need cattle, but horses like that one, we trade." With a nod of our heads, arrangements were made, and we headed back to camp.

"Samuel, I don't mind telling you, I was a bit concerned at first."

"Mathew, you did a great job; it never showed. I think we will make a lot of money together. I am proud to have you as a worthy business partner," Samuel stated sincerely.

We arrived in East St. Louis on the morning of August second. The cattle yards were filled, which meant we had to hold the drive outside of town for almost two weeks. The auction house had special pastures and watering holes arranged for situations such as these. Our work continued until there was room.

We had been out on the range for four months, and the wranglers were restless. After meeting with Conner, it was decided to allow two men rotations per day. One man could get himself in trouble, and more than two will cause problems. You find out the dedicated cowboys from the tenderfoots. There were a couple of new hands, and I needed to know to which party their dedication belonged to: the Lonestar or gunslinger.

Rotations began the following morning. The boys had four hour shifts, long enough to bathe and eat, or patron the saloon. Tenderfoots got the day shift, and the seasoned wranglers took the night spell. The experienced cowboys could handle the evening schedule.

Herds of cattle in such proximity to one another require twice the workload as out on the range. Bulls get the scent of females and want to breed, and they also yearn to fight for territory. Every cowboy must be on their toes.

Just before dawn, I was greeted by a tap on my left boot. "Are you Mathew Spinhirne?" Startled by the interaction, I grabbed my sidearm. "Don't do that. Slow and easy."

The sun's glare made it hard to see, but his badge glistened from the rays. I answered his question, "I am Mathew Spinhirne. What's going on, Marshal?"

"Can you please come with me? There are two men in my jail cell that say you are their boss," he stated.

The Marshal explained that during a card game last night one man was shot, and another stabbed. Both men were identified as the suspects.

"Marshal, I was not in town, but if they participated in these acts, there was a good reason. I can vouch for them both. They are respectable men."

"Well that may be, but the judge makes the final determination. The magistrate will be here in the morning," he said.

"What's the bail? Can I get them out?"

"Not when a man was killed. They stay here." I explained to the boys to sit tight, and I'd find Conner. We'd take care of this soon.

After searching for hours, I found Conner in the cattle market office trying to settle a dispute about the validity of our brand. A formal hearing was requested, and the accusations were absurd. None of our cows had been inspected yet. How could anyone complain about a problem? The whole mess with the boys last night and the brand issue left a bad taste in my mouth. Conner stayed at the office while I rode to camp and updated everyone on the happenings in town.

The campsite was empty and no one was around. The herd was quiet and undisturbed, but this was odd. Normally, there would be a note or someone here to relay messages. I figured the best place to start looking was the chuck wagon, but then out popped Stew. "Hi, Mathew. What are you doing back here? I thought you were in town." All the while, he was shifting his eyes sideways.

I answered, "Yes, I am headed there, but wanted to check and see if we needed any supplies."

"No, no I don't think so. Just take your time. We're alright here."

Now I knew there was trouble. Stew would never tell me to take my time, and we always needed supplies. I calmly placed my pistol back in its holster and hightailed it straight to the Marshal.

He greeted me outside his office. "I think we have a problem, Mathew. Come on in; I don't want anything to be overheard."

Once inside the office, he said, "Sit down, your men are safe, we had them moved. For the last several months we have had a serious situation with cattle rustling. The issue has been escalating quickly. Until now it's been a mystery, but when Conner came to see me earlier, I figured out their scam."

"Marshal, we will be happy to assist in any way possible, but first there is a problem out at my camp. Someone has my men hostage."

"Hostage? Are you sure?" he asked.

"Yes, Marshal. I need help. Can we get my boys and go?"

"Well, I guess we have no choice. My deputies are busy, and I don't think we should handle this alone."

With haste, the Marshal and I headed for the safe house, retrieved the men, loaded our guns, and headed for the herd.

Unsure of the circumstances, we chose to split into groups. We wanted to eliminate a possible ambush. The chuck wagon gave us the best cover while we scoped out the situation. Stew was tied up next to the buckboard, blindfolded and gagged. Behind the second wagon were the other four ranch hands. Since they were bound and gagged, there was no chance of them shouting and giving away our presence. The herd was still quiet and settled, which was a relief. There was a lot of money sitting in that pasture, but without caretakers, it would not take long before chaos ensued.

Hiding in the bushes out of sight, the Marshal stood guard as we freed my men. Believe me; they were mighty glad to see us come to their rescue. When it was all clear, we headed for shelter while they explained what happened.

It seemed five men came into camp with guns drawn, snatched Stew and then made him ring the dinner bell. It called in the boys without alerting them to their presence. All the hands gave the same basic story: five gunslingers on horseback moving small numbers of cattle to and fro. We stayed camouflaged while walking back to camp. Everyone regained their bearings and were ready for some payback.

"Guys, what happened to Samuel? Where is he?" I questioned them.

"Who is Samuel?" The Marshal asked.

"Well, sort of my business partner. At least was going to be," I answered angrily.

The Marshal told us he was heading back to town for answers. We were to meet at the Marshal's office in two hours. After he left, we separated and began to inspect the herd. All this nonsense raised suspicion, and Samuel disappearing during the middle of the crisis had me concerned. The thought of an elaborate scheme to sabotage the sale nagged me.

Teacup and I headed out across the pasture and noticed some riders in the distance, "Who is that, Teacup? Can you tell?" I asked him.

"Yeah, Mathew. Isn't that Samuel and Jessie?" he answered.

"I hope you're right, or we are in real trouble."

"Look, I'd know that horse anywhere," he said.

Sure enough, it was our men. Jessie found Samuel lying in the pasture. I flew off and ran toward him, "Are you alright? What happened?" I asked in a panic. "Go! Head for town, get the doc fast!" I yelled.

Samuel's injuries were severe; he could not ride alone. Jessie tied him to the saddle and headed for town with Steel in tow. I cleaned the wound and wrapped it with my bandana to help stop the bleeding, but he needed a doctor. Samuel's answers were difficult to ascertain, but we were able to put the bits and pieces together.

While monitoring this section of the drive, he noticed a calf separated from its cow. The division caused quite a stir for both baby and mama. As he worked to reunite the pair, a bull trampled him. The mystery was solved and the puzzle complete.

"Teacup, stay with Samuel, I have to go find the Marshal. The doc is on his way. Shoot anyone who gives you trouble. Do not hesitate, or I'll shoot you myself. Is that clear?" I told him.

"Yes sir, you have my word," he said.

The Marshal and Conner were at the jailhouse. "I know what's going on."

"Yes, Mathew, we figured it out as well. That is why I'm here. Come on; we'll fill you in on the plan to catch them," he told me.

In the market office, Conner and I would pretend to fight over money. I'd threaten to kill Conner for swindling the ranch, then storm out. Conner would approach the cattle inspector to offer him my cut if he padded the sale. He'd say he's tired of not making any money with me and wants a new partner. After the argument, I would head straight for the bar and spout off about my ex-partner and how I'd make him pay. Then, I'd make myself scarce for the night and let the plan play out.

By morning the word spread about our disagreement. The scheme worked better than planned. Instead of Conner approaching the inspector, he reached out. Once they made the final arrangements, the Marshal had enough evidence to arrest everyone involved.

The scam was simplistic but brilliant. Cattle in the stockyards are weighed and sold by the pound. The rustlers round up the largest animals in each herd; each one is weighed by the inspectors, who document the sale docket.

When the rancher's head rotates for auction, each sale price is written in another book. Ranch owners are paid from the fake report, thus leaving a difference in payment. In return, it's split among all parties involved.

The stockyards bring chaos to town, creating diversions. So, no one noticed the real issues behind the scenes. All inspectors involved were ordered to repay the funds and arrested to stand trial. The market staff was fired, along with any ranchers participating in the scheme. Plus, their privileges were revoked from any further auction sales.

The Marshal paid his respects for our help in settling the scandal. Since the issue was resolved, most of us headed for home. Some of the men, restless and exhausted, requested to stay in town for a few days. Since raising cattle was now in the past, I granted their wish. The rest of us sought peaceful bliss.

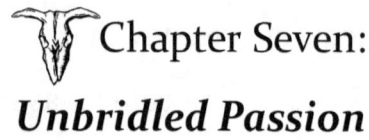 Chapter Seven:

Unbridled Passion

A cattle drive is the most grueling experience one can endure. The labor of moving herds numbering in the thousands from one place to another in short spans ages any man. Time is of the essence to have good returns, but safety takes a toll as the end nears. A blessing is traveling from start to finish with minimal occurrences. One death is considered normal, but not in my book.

The exhaustion takes hold, and we run on pure adrenaline for the last several weeks. Profit is the motivator. The men are grateful when their pay increases and bonuses come. It's difficult to keep quality help when you do not pay them adequately. Being concerned for the ranch's success is draining, but this year our prayers were answered: we incurred record profits at auction.

The trek home was calm and peaceful; reveling in the earnings made the trip worthwhile. Each man handled themselves admirably under the circumstances. We had a rocky start, but they pulled it together. In respect of our accomplishment, a two-night stay in town seemed appropriate. It gave everyone time to unwind and cut loose before the long journey. The stopover delayed our departure an extra few days, but knowing ranch work never ceases, it sealed my fate as Dad's replacement.

We arrived home on a Tuesday. The leaves on the trees had started to change color. A crisp breeze chilled the air, shadowed by the inner mask of summer waning. Sheer elation filled my heart as the doom of chasing cattle for a living vanished.

In utter tranquility as I strolled up the drive, I saw someone waiting for me on the porch. At this distance discerning their identity was difficult, although the figure raised my suspicions. The image stirred places that gave reason to doubt the intentions of a gentleman.

Sarah so captivated my thoughts that the world stopped. I had visions of our bodies entangled in a fiery passion. It's a sensation that makes your heart beat to live another day and experience the pleasure of one more encounter. The feeling was like the thrill of chasing a wild cow through the thickets, sweat beading on your brow and adrenaline pumping for more.

She wiped the perspiration from my jaw as a gleaming smile appeared on her face. Sarah was pleased with the state of mind her presence caused. But, when the intensity of our embrace claimed her soul, a bead of sweat rolled down the center of her bosom. Her cheeks flushed with a brilliant shade of pink; the innocent women delved into the intimate nature of love.

We drew apart, our passions building for eternal matrimony. The evening found me on the porch reveling in emotion, waiting for the dinner bell.

If my stomach had not been demanding nourishment, it might have gone unnoticed. Real home-cooked food was something I'd been craving all afternoon, well, besides a bath and some clean clothes. The adoration of my bride was put on hold.

Our meal was a sensational supper. We ate until we were stuffed, like pigs at a trough. Bathing in hot, soapy water was an equally tantalizing treat. During these cattle drives, dirt begins to fill every crevasse of your body. If you have a chance to bathe, it may be in a stream or soaked from a thundershower. Wash tubs are not an option. The only yearning that caused excitement now was slumber, an irrefutable offer.

When I entered the house, the feeling of being home hit me. I had missed this place. The gentle sensation further enhanced my gratitude. It illustrated my intense need for rest. The longing over, sleep became my captor. Thoughts of an engaging nights peace overwhelmed me. The last and final step proceeded. In the summer blankets evacuate the scene, but with the chill of fall it makes them necessary. Otherwise, comfort is preferable on top of the covers.

The bed was complete and untouched since our departure for the cattle drive, it became a perfect image of serene relaxation. A solace of homey delight. It was difficult to focus in the dim light of the room, but something caught my eye. Instinct urged me to get a lamp, but that meant shifting my eyes.

"How can I reach the lantern and expose the scene at the same time?" I pondered the situation. "Well, whatever I decide, I have to be quick."

Eager to uncover the monster's identity, my thoughts shifted again, "What if…. there are multiple fiends gathered under the covers? How will I eliminate them all?"

I paused, formulating my choices. Either expose the sheets and face the risks, or siesta on the floor one more night. Once considered, the decision was easy: remove the blanket and confront the beast in my bed.

I reached slowly, so as not to scare the furry creature while inspecting the area for his whereabouts. My pursuit drove to end this conflict. Sleep sauntered, moseying away from the scene. Feverishly, I scanned the sheets; then a glimpse of something gray under the pillow. His beady little eyes stared at me intently. He was taunting me, knowing full well who had the upper hand. The battle was set, his offense against my defense. We gazed at each other, daring the other to make the first move. Steady… the plan commenced. In a second, the production began. Children would tell the tale throughout eternity.

Somehow this pest was leaving. I raised my arm, leaning over the mattress. A little mouse would not delay slumber any longer. Intent on the conclusion, I didn't notice my opponent had snagged an opportunity. Gray fur sailed across the gap. He hit my chest and slid to the lower reaches of my long Johns, and distress welled up inside me immediately. The frantic fussing of a fool, I danced around anxious to be rid of him. Distracted by the experience, I was ignorant of the plotting scheme outside the house.

While our affair lingered, the memoirs were being written. My ranting extended as I continued to shake and jerk, trying to release the monster from my trousers. As I gasped for air, he finally broke free. The nightmare ended, he escaped doom. The vermin scurried to a small hole in the corner the room. I'd been duped by a mouse.

My plan of ending this situation quickly and peacefully was obliterated. A mouse left me panting; it was unbelievable. I scanned the room for other inhabitants, but my attention was diverted by the half-pulled shade. Still, under the pretext, my escapes weren't exposed I sauntered to the window, getting a sense of the situation. I peered through the pane, looking for any gawkers, and my hope was squashed. The looky-loos rolled on the ground with laughter. I wanted to stay in character and remain tranquil, but found the barrage of riddling to be nonexistent when exiting the front door. The commotion died abruptly.

Perched on the porch in long Johns and stocking feet, the bystanders slunk back to their beds for the night. The acknowledgment of my actions was hilarious. If the roles were reversed, my eyes would have peered through the window pane. The contemplation of revenge seized my attention for the moment. Any time wasted on explaining my predicament was moot. Although, if I succeeded it would end the barrage of ridicule that would chase me to the grave.

It became clear that sleeping on the floor was the best course of action. The only concern that remained was, "Would the rodent seek revenge during my unconscious state of slumber?"

As I paced to slow my heart rate, sheer exhaustion came over me. The choice of staying awake vanished. In seconds, the sounds of my snoring filled the house.

Stew had a firm grasp of the bell handle; I nearly jumped out of my skin. The clanging splintered my head as it chimed, but relief came when the mouthwatering delight warmed my veins. As the sensuous fluid flowed through my body, I heard a knock.

"Mathew… are you awake? It's me, Rusty," he stated in an uncertain voice.

My motives, needless to say remained a mystery, but the previous night's incident left Rusty suspicious.

"Please come in. What do you need?" responded. The jovial tension tickled my fancy when he entered.

"Um…. Mathew, the horses have been fed, do you want to doctor them this morning?"

I sat static in my chair, observing him quiver with anticipation. He continued to shudder, waiting for a response as he examined my facial expression for some alteration. Then finally it poured out, "Mathew I will never laugh again, please don't hurt me... Just say something," he pleaded.

I was speechless; laughter was expelled from every fiber of my core. Rusty withstood the torment longer than expected. His patience extended my guffawing. Nodding yes was the only form of dialogue I could convey.

He hurried out the door, but his haste only encouraged my laughter. My ribs ached, and I flailed about from hysterics. All of this anxiety over the previous events made my torment came to life.

The day ran like a broken clock. Our chores piled high while stamina waned. We all needed a good night's sleep. Sheer fatigue eliminated any trepidations over last night's escapades. I was grateful when dawn emerged, leaving me well rested and prepped for a day's work.

A new chapter opened today. I greeted Stew as he exited the bunkhouse, with an expression that every man understands at some point. He saw the same look. A nod and smile were enough of a reply; no amount of coffee or breakfast would drop this feeling of urgency.

Life has a way of stopping short, leaving you hanging off the edge of a cliff with no escape route. I'd been in these boots many times, and panicking will only exasperate the problem. It's imperative to always have a backup plan. The only thing we can control is how we handle each situation. Circumstances in our path are unique so every solution must also be distinctive. The type of resolution we choose may not always exist. Sometimes, you make do with what's available.

The solution guided us down a long, narrow path lined with rocks, winding up the mountainside, through a row of trees that intertwined with each other, making the sky disappear. The air is scented with pine sap, a cool breeze tickles your face, and birds chirp a catchy melody to keep your feet moving along the trail. The hillside trek is as much of a therapeutic adventure as the destination. At the top, it opens to a clearing stuffed with wildflowers and grasses of all descriptions. In the center is a wrought-iron fence embedded in a stone wall. Rows of small gray headstones follow the wall, leaving room in the middle for a large white cross. The symbol greets people, inviting them to enter.

Today was an exceptional day. The sunrise turned the majestic cross fire red. It was an incredible sight. My trepidations seemed meaningless. Mesmerized by beauty, the scene left me immobile. This plot of land was fertile with knowledge and wisdom. It holds the remains of departed family. A genuine peace permeated the air; their spirits soothed the apprehensions of life. A oneness with the world occupied my soul once again.

Belayed by my journey to the cemetery, Stew prepped a horse and buggy.
Although my nervousness passed, anxious emotions stirred. A scheduled arrangement at the church was made for one o'clock sharp; I arrived a few minutes late. All the guests were seated except Sarah. She waited patiently on the front steps for my arrival.

"Is everything alright, Mathew?" she asked.

"Everything is fine. I will explain later," I replied.

Our entrance was met with applause. We stood in the entryway and gazed upon the parishioners. Their warmth calmed my apprehensions. The preacher welcomed us with open arms at the altar. His sermon faded, and any questions I had ceased. Our thoughts merged; at this point, the wedding was just a formality. The emotions were exhilarating, my nervous trepidations unwarranted. Passion excited my soul; I was hooked.

Our work day concluded, but the afternoon was a comfortable change of venue. The camp settled in with a warm cup of coffee and a seat by the fire. My heated twirling mug of black gold excelled my yearnings to settle a debt, retribution sat at the table. The stories circled around the fire, encompassing everyone, saving me for last.

I lingered a moment, extending their curiosity, taunting my cohorts. All eyes were tuned to me, and no one suspected anything. I swallowed, putting a halt to the laughter for the meantime. It would be the perfect ending to the day.

I began the account: "It was a sultry summer night, the air thick as butter. A woman appeared from the shadows, walking towards a motel. The illuminating street lights exposed the fire red material of her dress, gently formed around her hourglass figure. My pace slowed, entranced by the well of desire her presence created. Our eyes met with the intensity of a bull defending his territory. She stopped… holding her position, provoking my advances. The delicate skin of her bosom pushed beyond the confinements of her dress. Temptation reigned. My thoughts betrayed the intentions of a gentleman. The fixation left me paralyzed, but she continued to move towards me, her alluring smile, our gazed locked.

"We found ourselves captivated, yearning for intimate contact. The long-awaited cravings warmed her delicate lips, which carried us to the room. Our attraction resulted in unspeakable acts throughout the night. The morning left me wanting more of the Spanish senorita named Consuela. As I scanned the room, searching for her presence, it was empty. The passion in my memories was all that remained."

My story left a silence that only roosters crowing at dawn could break. In fact, no one even noticed the fire was no more than smoldering ashes, and the chilly morning breeze cooled the lower reaches of our trousers, thus finalizing my revenge.

Chapter Eight:
The Cowboy's Partner

In the last a year, unexpected pleasures had presented themselves without notice. The same graces that enrich our life, every second they exist. Those chapters grow and mature into something blessed. The progression shared between people requires no knowledge or understanding; oneness is natural.

My journey to church cleared the path from past to present. A fundamental basis of honesty and truth enables intimacy, and the open arms of marriage awaited my presence. Seeing the chapel upon my arrival left me mesmerized. The sunlight warmed my face; birds serenaded me, a gentle breeze fanned my face, and peace filled the air.

Bells in the steeple were chiming to announce the event. My attendance was mandatory. An angel in white appeared. Embraced by her father's arm, they proceeded down the aisle. Her yearning echoed within my soul.

With my hand extended, we turned to approach the altar. As the words emanated throughout the room, everything went silent. Only the echo of our thoughts resonated, and emotions flooded the room. Love unbridled, untouched by humanity, left me petrified. Staggered by the occurring events, every fiber of my being wanted to run. Then, a gentle squeeze from the woman who would become my wife squashed my fears with a single touch. The parish stood, applauding the announcement.

"I now pronounce you man and wife. Mathew, you may kiss the bride," the preacher stated.

The cheers rang throughout the church. Our family and friends saw an incredible grace from God: the joining of two hearts.

"Mathew," she said. "You do not need fear the unknown alone. The heart in your body now beats as one with mine. So, no matter how far our travels take us, I will always be there with you." Her words resonated with me, leaving me speechless.

Stepping into the world as husband and wife felt incredible. Our journey as newlyweds began. We waved goodbye and blew kisses to our loved ones.

Morning found me noticing the bright rays of sunlight shining through the bedroom window. They exposed the beautiful woman lying next to me. The passion we created during the night left her in slumber, her figure draped in the sheets. My mind wandered to images of the moonlight glistening across her skin when our ardent intentions took hold.

The world appeared pristine this morning. The past seemed unimportant, our future was bright and willing to fulfill our dreams. Life displayed images that are relevant to being married; it was a relishing adventure.

 Chapter Nine:

An Unexpected Presence

Our trek home found the wheels of fate bearing gifts from divine forces. To seek justice would endanger the well being of a lifelong partner. Principled gentlemen will be tempted by aggression, due to the repulsive actions of men. Some people obtain control from the exploitation of others.

Sometimes, travel in midsummer cannot be avoided, but leaving early in the day is essential. Survival is the highest concern during the heated months. We boarded the stage at daybreak to reach our home by nightfall.

The driver took an unfamiliar route that morning but advised us it was a better choice during the summer months. Horses and people get overheated, increasing the necessity for breaks. The road ran next to two large cattle ponds and several oversized cedar trees for shade. Most stages start the horses at a steady gallop for several miles, and then slow to an easy trot. It gives them time to cool. A varied speed allows the horses to travel most of the day without switching animals.

The first stop is always for lunch. Faster travel is preferred in the mornings when it's cooler. Breaks provide enough time to eat, use the restroom, and stretch your legs, and the distance between towns determines the number of rest periods.

During our first break, the driver noticed a damaged wheel on the stage. Our only choice was to slow down and ensure the safety of everyone involved, which extended the length of our journey. I soon realized everything happens for a reason. The added time showed the divine intervention in the following events.

Boredom settled in at this pace and sleep overtook me. I used the corner of the stage for stability from the jarring ride. However, as road conditions deteriorated, sleep became impossible. Soon, the driver told us that a break was scheduled in a few minutes. The announcement was delightful, a vacation from the stage. As we approached the stopping point, a sound echoed off the canyon that any cowboy learns to understand at a young age.

The cry resonated through the stage, bringing it to a screeching halt. We scanned the horizon for signs of altercations, but nothing appeared obvious. The screams continued to fill the air, and shivers ran up my spine. Once outside, the driver located the problem and we saw a scene no man wants to witness, especially when womenfolk are present. We instructed everyone to stay put while we investigated.

We crawled up the pond bank for vantage of the scene. With no thought to our safety, we trekked across the field to capture the riders wreaking havoc on their unsuspecting victims. They were so preoccupied with their merry-making our presence came as a surprise. We were granted the next blessing in disguise and divine intervention kept us safe once again. Our unexpected approach left the revelers caught with their pants down.

As we approached, guns cocked and drawn, our demands were taken seriously: "Boys, I will say this one time, and after that there will be no more talking. You will throw your guns on the ground and dismount. Then move over to my partner."

The men heard anger and realized the sincerity of our command, and neither one argued. Once both men dismounted and walked to my colleague, I explained what would happen next: "Sit on the ground; we'll tie your hands. When we make it to town, I'll advise the Marshal of your whereabouts. If I had my way, you'd rot out here in the desert." Silence ensued.

These two men had lassoed an old mustang mare and dragged her around the muddy watering hole while she was giving birth. Then after her feet became stuck in the mud and she fell, they continued to drag her. The rope cut through the artery in her neck. By the time we reached the mare she had perished from her injuries. We stood with tears in our eyes. The idea of eliminating both men weighed heavy on our minds. Enraged by the incident, we lingered for a minute, trying to regain our composure. The scene was horrific and passing this information along to the other passengers would be difficult.

I plopped on the ground, disgusted and wanting to murder the men responsible. My partner stood next to me, considering the same. Our intended delay allowed for the miracle of catching the men in the act. The colt, lying in the mud, kicked and called for his mother.

Engrossed by the present situation, my yearning to eliminate the men dissolved. I yelled, "Yahoo! Come on." We both made a mad dash to the foal.

The colt remained in the amniotic sac, so getting him air was imperative. Once clear, drying him was essential. In nature, the mare licks the foals clean to eliminate the smell, which helps to keep predators away. That was not possible. Cloth being scarce, my shirt became the best option. We were both joyous at being able to save a life. It worked like a charm; the foal was dry and clean. But, in the midst of the commotion, we failed to think about nursing the colt. Then Dan, the stage driver, had a marvelous idea, "We'll get a canteen and milk the mare."

"Ok," I replied. "But how do we get the colt to nurse from a canteen?"

"Let's cross that bridge when we come to it. Why don't you stay with the colt? I'll fetch a canteen and be right back."

Dan wasted no time retrieving the item we needed. In the mud pit, holding the colt and staring at the image before my eyes, my rage built. If I wasn't protecting this foal, those boys might not live another day on this earth. Payback for this repugnant act was pending.

Dan returned, carrying the canteen, but brought a welcome surprise. "Mathew, she insisted on coming to help."

"Good, Dan, we could use it. It won't be easy getting him out of the mud."

The muck was knee high in the middle of the waterhole and carrying the colt out was not an option. So, we stood in a line. Each person passed the foal to the next, and then moved to the opposite end until we were free of the pond. It took several passes to reach the edge. The incident left us covered in mud and angry, but the chore was for a worthwhile cause. He was raring to go once freed.

We still had the dilemma of how to nurse him, but then Sarah thought of a brilliant plan: "Mathew, we can tear strips from my petticoat and soak them in the milk for the colt to suckle." She stood and stared at me for a minute, waiting for my response.

I smiled and said, "Well… start tearing! I'll pour the milk in my hat and hold the pieces while he nurses." You can always tell a good cowboy by how well his hat holds water. Our strategy worked. The colt nursed and filled his belly.

After we got him settled in with Sarah, I rode up top with the driver. It gave the passengers more room, but our added weight slowed our travel. Mid-day was in full force as we got going, and the heat was dehydrating us. We agreed it was best to send someone ahead for help. Our break had given the horses plenty of time to rest, so losing one did not affect travel.

We got back on track as soon as possible. I was glad to be riding up top. Being able to talk with Dan kept boredom at bay. The last time I slept, all hell broke loose, and I'd had enough excitement for one day.

The sun was setting low in the western sky when we noticed riders. We waited with bated breath until we could determine their identities. It was the Marshal and two deputies.

The Marshal dismounted and told us, "I am grateful you are okay, we were starting to worry. The stage departed on time. I must admit, if I didn't know Dan and you, Matthew, I would never believe such an outlandish story. Where's the colt? Oh... another stage is coming behind us to take you and your littlest traveler home."

When the Marshal saw Sarah sitting with the colt in her lap, he stepped back, shaking his head. I knew that once he witnessed the site where the incident took place, his blood would boil as much as ours. He never spoke of his encounter with the two men responsible, and I never asked. It was between them and the Lord.

Dan insisted on coming with us in the replacement stage; he was committed to the end. His company was appreciated. A respectable man worthy of praise. Dan kicked the horses in gear and headed straight for the ranch. He dropped us at home and took the passengers to town. The Marshal sent word so that they could prepare milk for our passenger.

Rusty and Walter had rounded up that old cow who had escaped capture to take over the role of nurse mare. "What?" I asked, "that old heifer? She'll kill this colt."

Walter replied, "Mathew, trust me; that colt will be like one of her own. She

saved one of our horses a long time ago.
Nursed it after the mare died. Let him
go… he'll be fine."

Another miracle dropped right in our laps.
Just as Walter predicted, she nuzzled that
colt and turned for him to nurse. By the
next morning, her utter was full. The only
drawback was, that old cow was in
protective mode. His taming would wait
until she weaned him in nine months.

The horrific sight witnessed that day
forever remained in my mind. Its picture
silences any man privy to the tale. But, the
encounter did not leave tears of sorrow,
but rather the strength of life in our hearts.
We were blessed with a great joy named
Spirit.

Chapter Ten:

Matched Ponies

The transformations in the business were exhilarating. The stock pens, cattle shoots, and wild cow chases were gone. Ranch hands found the change of venue a dream come true. Horse taming is the opposite end of the spectrum compared to cattle, but every man jumped at the chance to learn. We still had herds on the property, but with one major difference: they were for training horses to work cattle. It covered both ends of the horse business to increase profits and maintain my father's reputation. The round-up this year would be to sell horse stock to the ranchers, not cattle for market.

In the middle of the year, the summer heat brings things to a halt. Ranch work is completed early, at dawn or in the evening before dark. It left time to relax and breathe. The ranch can run on a skeleton crew. After round-up, some men go home, others visit their families, and the rest use the time to make extra money doing odd jobs. This year, with the cattle numbers low and the stock in pasture, Samuel and I planned a trip.

Samuel headed the excursion, and our destination remained secret. He refused to reveal the details; the only information he shared was that we were heading to a small area in the southern part of the country. A region filled with horses, he said it was a place we could call home. The excitement burst through every pore. Our journey took several weeks, and all we did was ride and enjoy the scenery.

Once in sight of our destination, Samuel explained the reason for this expedition. After leaving the east coast in the late 1700s, his family moved out west. They liked the climate and settled. In their caravan were several thoroughbred stallions. After raising horses on the east coast for many years, Samuel's father wanted to spread his bloodlines throughout the country. The idea sounded grand, but horse breeds are different on the east coast than in the western half of the country. To sell, the local broncobusters a large horse bred for speed, would be like teaching a cat not to chase mice. They did, however, find the speed of these thoroughbreds preferable to the mustangs available in the west. A proposal was born.

The farther south we traveled, the more their similarities grabbed my attention. Horses in this area were short, wide, and had beautiful heads and broad set eyes. Samuel nodded his head when I stated the obvious, "I'm getting to that part soon."

His father bred the thoroughbred stallions with mustang mares in the area, which produced a well-rounded horse with the characteristics they wanted and needed to work wild cattle. Yet, one attribute escaped their awareness: the ability to create tremendous amounts of speed for the distance of a quarter-mile. It led to a horse that worked cattle all week and competed in match races on the weekends. The cattle industry is not always profitable for the small rancher, but competitive match races supplement their income.

Some of the local horses won so many races no one would compete against them, so the owners quit racing and went in search of new competitors. This was why Samuel trekked west to find new bloodlines and breed his racing stock. He knew there was a future in raising quarter-milers. The way to start was to enter one of the largest match races in the country. If we proved the stallion's speed, that would force the contestants to buy their quarter-milers from us if they wanted to win.

The challenge of winning races was acceptable and one of the main reasons Samuel had sought us out was due to a match race. Since the better part of my life was spent chasing wild cows, the experience was exhilarating. The only struggle would be between the two mounts we rode.

Told by the Passenger of a Spotted Stallion Determined to Win.

Stretched across the start line, the horses stood nose to nose. Seated atop my mount, trembling with anticipation, my eyes peeled on the road ahead, waiting, frozen in position. Time slowed, and the seconds ticked by as we sat prepped to hear the gunshot that started the race. The upcoming forecast caused my decision to ease deep in the saddle, push hard against the stirrups and grasp the reins to stay in the seat. There were no misgivings about my mounts intentions to win.

The gunshot rang out, **"Bang!"**

Hunched forward, muscles tight, impulse drove us over the start line. We moved into the front section of the herd with ease. Only the sound of hooves could be heard over the crowd screaming as the horses passed the grandstands.

As the race charged on, the horses gathered in a group, and nameless faces blurred as my horse's speed increased down the dirt path. The thrust of his hindquarters pushed against my body as we were propelled forward. It forced me to take a tight grip on the reins for safe passage to the finish line.

With each stride, the momentum flattened my horse's back, lengthening the stride, driving us closer to the end. The muscles in my arms ached trying to keep my post. Gripping the reins for balance, Cash pulled tighter as our speed increased. The finish line drew near, and no amount of agony endured by the rider would bring an end to our trek. His passion for winning raged.

The roar of the horse's breath forced from the nostrils sounded like an angry bull attempting trepidation upon his captures. Sweat rolled down his body, frothing from the edges of the saddle blanket as we stampeded down the final stretch. With every inch we gained, his drive to win caused an increase in stamina, moving us closer to victory.

Triumph in sight, we pushed towards the end, our determination remained strong as we proceeded to our destiny. Only the two quarter-milers who were meant to change history would cross the finish line, noses even.

Anna provides it all as if you are in the saddle along for the journey. Her rare books bring the readers joy from nearly every genre they can appreciate. She exuberantly brings the image and sentiments of the west to full life throughout the storyline. Yet, at the core of Judd's work is a black stallion who engages life into every aspect of the book. Haystack fills children's minds with wonder as he interacts with Marshal Spur and the Outrider Gang, to the mild minored young steed who brings

Adam to new levels of learning in his life. Then he is brilliantly portrayed as a beautiful Appaloosa stallion in the Broncobuster as Cash.

Anna is one of the greatest novelists and a freelance ghostwriter is known for equestrian professionalism in every genre. Her young adult fiction novels and all books bring joy to the readers.

Lizzy is the founder of Writers Publishing House/Ghost Writer Media, who writes under her pen name Anna Elizabeth Judd, a solid publishing firm with more than a decade of assisting clients will their publishing needs. She has a BA in fine arts, with a minor in Equine Science. On the side, she studied at Scottsdale Art Institute under Robert 'Shoofly' Shufelt.

Lizzy writes books, which considering this website, makes perfect sense. She is best known for ghostwriting various best sellers in all genres. Along with her novels based on the initial part of her working career, horse training. As she understands the importance of family values, Lizzy chose a pen name borrowed from her family tree, Anna Elizabeth Judd.

When not absorbed in writing for clients, Lizzy can be found hiking, biking, or any outside activity. Although she does not train horses any longer, their spirits will always be a part of her soul. As a passionate entrepreneur Lizzy understands the importance of exemplary customer service, it is the basis for any successful business. In this case, Writers Publishing House was founded on the idea that the focus must be on the client's success. She believes, "Everyone should profit from their passion."

If you want to know more about publishing a book, please visit her website at https://writerspublishinghouse.com where you can contact her about starting your book project today.
Anna's Books: annaelizabethjudd.com

- The Power of Thought
- IAuthor – Social Media Marketing Guide

- The Handbook of Horsemanship
- The Broncobusters
- The Hourglass of el Diablo

- Marshal Spur and the Outlaw
- The Boy Who Couldn't Talk
- Spur Up! – Music Album
- Hey, Hay Learn Your ABC's
- Learn Your ABCs with Haystack

- A Distant Calling
- Skimmer's Adventure

www.ingramcontent.com/pod-product-compliance
Lightning Source LLC
Chambersburg PA
CBHW071602110726
47908CB00007B/2206